NO LIMIT

Gina,
When the stakes are
high, it's all or
nothing!
♡ LPDwn

NO LIMIT

An **ARMED AND DANGEROUS** novel

L.P. DOVER

No Limit

L.P. Dover

Copyright 2015 by L.P. Dover

Editor: Victoria Schmitz at Crimson Tide Editorial

Cover Design by: Regina Wamba www.maeidesign.com

Model: Josh McCann

Interior designed and formatted by

E.M.
TIPPETTS
BOOK DESIGNS

www.emtippettsbookdesigns.com

I'd like to dedicate this book to my dad, Jerry Moore. Out of everyone in my family, he has been one of my biggest supporters. No Limit wouldn't have been written without his help. A huge thank you goes out to him and I hope he knows how much I love him.

PROLOGUE

JASON

"You found me."

If there was ever a moment when I needed to keep my wits about me, it was now. But how could I do that when I wanted nothing more than to snap the man's neck in front of me; to make him bleed like he did the families he murdered.

"Did you think I wouldn't?" I spat through clenched teeth. His file flashed through my mind, the pictures of the carnage he left behind . . . those children. My blood boiled.

He was poised, ready to fight to the death by the look in his eyes. "I guess it was only a matter of time."

His name was Michael Bruxton, a computer analyst

with skills matching my own. But he had a sick hobby that cost the lives of three families over the past two weeks. I spent day and night searching for him, and now I found the bastard.

We circled each other in the rundown, abandoned warehouse he'd holed up in while on the run. On the floor were tokens he stole from his victims. The baby doll with a bright pink dress caught my attention first. My whole body shook with rage. "How could you do it, you sick fuck?"

His eyes sparkled. "It's like putting paint to canvas." He looked down at the things he collected and smiled. "Their pleas for help were music to my ears."

Flashes of the children laying in their own blood, their lives taken from them at such a young age plagued my mind. They were innocent, along with their parents who only wanted to protect them. A man like him deserved to die a slow, painful death . . . and I was going to make sure that happened.

Lunging for him, we went down to the dirty floor, his head slamming against the concrete. He tried to punch me and missed. I couldn't hear anything other than the blood rushing through my veins. Pinning him with my weight, I punched him over and over, the feel of his bones crunching beneath my fist. I didn't know the families who were killed, but I fought for them, bringing their murderer to justice.

The sick fuck spit to clear his throat, blood dribbling down his cheek, and laughed. "I love it when they fight back." He pushed his arousal into me and groaned.

Jesus Christ. Grabbing his neck, I squeezed and snuffed his next words out. "You get off on pain you perverted son of a bitch?" I picked up a brick from nearby and raised it high. "Let's see how you like this." As hard as I could, I slammed it down on his face. "You said screams were music to your ears," I yelled into the silence. "Where are the screams now, you bitch?" I slammed the brick back down on his mutilated face over and over again, trying to unsee the pictures of the flayed bodies he'd left behind.

Throwing the brick across the floor, I got up and surveyed the scene, breathing hard. "Now you can't hurt anyone ever again."

"Got anything new comin' up?" Blake asked, leaning against the doorframe.

Strapping on my holster, I shook my head. After everything that happened with Bruxton, I needed a break. "I hope not. You?"

Jaw tight, he trudged into my office, gray eyes full of turmoil. "Actually, I'm headin' out for good. I just wanted to say goodbye."

"What the hell are you talking about? Are you skipping town or quitting the team?"

Blake Evans and the rest of the guys on our team were the best undercover agents in the country. We'd already lost a couple people, including my sister who decided to move away to California to settle down. We couldn't afford to lose another skilled agent.

A small smile splayed across his face as he sat down. "I'm still going to be a part of the team. This is my life. I'll just be living it somewhere else."

"Where to?"

"Wyoming. My grandfather passed away and left me his ranch. I figured I'd go since nothing's really keeping me here. I'm single, and we're always traveling with the job. I'm never in Charlotte that much anyway."

"No shit. I think this is the first week in months I've been able to sit back and relax." I stared at him and chuckled. "Blake Evans turned cowboy. I never would've thought it."

He got to his feet. "Me neither, but it'll sure be interesting. How about we get one last drink together at Second Street before I go?"

"Sounds good, bro. I was just about to head out." We got halfway to the door when my cell phone rang. I looked down at my phone and walked back to my desk. "It's the Chief of Police from Vegas." So much for the break I wanted. Leaning against my desk, I answered the call. "Ryan Griffin, to what do I owe the pleasure?"

"No pleasure in this call, son. Are you still at the station?"

"I was just getting ready to leave. What do you need?"

Sounding tired, he sighed. "I sent you some files. Take a look at them for me."

Blake took a seat while I sat back down behind my computer. It didn't take long for it to boot back up and when it did, I found the files. "All right, I have the files opened up." The first one was a woman who was found dead two months prior, followed by two other murder victims and one who was missing. "What the fuck is this?"

"Whoever this fucker is, he's cutting them, strangling them, and then leaving them on the side of the road."

I waved Blake over. "Take a look at this," I whispered, holding the phone away. While he sat down, I moved back. "Did it all start two months ago with this first woman, or have you had similar cases?"

"Nope, all new. We've had eyewitnesses give us descriptions of the people these women were last seen with—all high rollers of Sin City. No one wants to talk. All we're getting are dead ends. I need someone on the inside who doesn't look like a cop. My people can't get close enough."

Blake moved out of the way and I glanced at the

pictures one last time before closing them out. "I'll be there soon," I said, hanging up.

"That's some really nasty shit going on out there," Blake stated.

Anger boiled in my veins. The pictures of those women were going to forever be ingrained in my mind. "Yes, it is, and I'm going to make sure I find the fucker responsible."

CHAPTER 1

JASON

(Three Months Later)

"Going out again?" Ryan grumbled through the phone.

"That's the plan. I can't exactly do much sitting on my ass."

"One would think that's what you've been doing since you haven't figured out shit. Please tell me you have something . . . anything other than the thousands you've won."

Clenching my teeth, I took a deep breath. "I've given you more than what you were able to come up with on your own. For three months now, I've kicked ass at each casino and learned every single game. I have a name out there, but nothing's going to make these guys seek me out. I'm nothing to them."

Unfortunately, two more girls had shown up dead. Both were professional escorts from the same agency, which happened to be run by Ronnie Chatfield, a female pimp. I had yet to speak to her, but was determined to seek her out. The woman was invisible. On her website, it said the ranch was temporarily closed for business, yet more of their girls were disappearing.

The women were beautiful, some fuller than others, and way more expensive than the drugged out prostitutes you'd see on the street. These women were for the elite. Other than that, I did know what my suspects looked like, what their names were, where they worked, who their families were . . . basically, it was tracking them that was a complete bitch.

"But at least you're enjoying the money in the meantime, right?" he scoffed.

"Kiss my fucking ass. I'm here to help you out. I don't have to be here. If anyone wants to get this case solved quickly, it's me. I'm ready to get the hell away from this place."

Ryan huffed and the line grew silent. I had made a shit ton of money, but that was because I was good at the games. To get in with the high rollers, I had no choice but to learn. As a reward, the casinos offered me free rooms and other amenities. I was living like a king. There was no denying I enjoyed it, but my full focus was on the case, nothing else.

"Look, I hate to be a dick, but the FBI is breathing down my neck. If you don't figure something out soon, they're going to intervene."

I snorted. "I'd like to see them get as far as I have."

"Either way, they will show up. I just want you to be prepared. I've worked with some of those douchebags before."

"As long as they stay out of my way, I'm fine."

"I can already tell you now . . . they won't."

CHAPTER 2

JASON

One Week Later

"Mr. Avery, would you like another gin and tonic?"

I looked up and smiled. "That'd be great." The night was young and I already had over two hundred grand in chips. Ryan's words about the FBI butting in had been nagging on me all week.

"Is there anything else I can get you?" the sultry waitress asked, biting her lower lip. She stuck her tits out, showing me the hardened nipples through her white shirt. Her hand slid up my thigh and my dick twitched.

Groaning, I pushed her hand away. I almost wanted to take what she was offering, slide away to a back room and fuck her senseless. She wasn't exactly the type of woman I'd go for, but a dark room could do wonders. It'd been an eternity since I'd had a good fuck. "Sorry, sweetheart. I don't have time to play tonight."

"Maybe next time?" she asked, sounding hopeful.

I kissed her hand and winked. "We'll see."

Tossing back the gin and tonic, I grabbed my chips and started for the floor. I had played every single game so much it bored me. The stakes were all the same, there was no competition. Going through the motions, I spent the next three hours going from table to table. It wasn't until the brush of a hand on my shoulder pulled me out of my monotony. I thought it was the waitress trying her luck again, but it wasn't.

"Do you mind if I join you?" Her hair was a deep red and in soft curls past her shoulders, and her eyes were the clearest blue I'd ever seen.

"What's your name?" I asked, staring at her tight black dress.

She took a seat beside me, grinning wide. "Ariel, and yours?"

By the look in her seductive blue eyes I knew she was lying. I held out my hand. "I'm Eric. Want to board my ship?"

Catching the reference, she shook my hand. "Well played. But I'd be more than happy to ride on your ship."

"Normally I'd say all aboard, but now is not a good time," I said, getting to my feet.

Smirking, she got up and let go of my hand. "Pity. I was hoping to have some fun tonight."

"Oh, I'm sure there are plenty of gentlemen here who could use your services."

"Am I that obvious?" she challenged, regarding me with narrowed eyes.

"It's of no concern to me either way." But before I could turn away, an idea sparked. Looking at the red haired vixen, she was exactly the type of person I needed. Unfortunately, the men I was searching for weren't there. "Actually, I may have a proposition for you."

"What kind of proposition?"

I pulled out one of my cards and wrote my number on it. "It might be dangerous, so I understand if you don't want to. But you look like the kind of girl who'd be up for a challenge."

She took my card and smiled, her eyes lit with humor. "You have no idea."

"All you have to do is give me a call tomorrow morning."

"What kind of money you talking?"

I tapped her chin and winked. "Don't worry, you'll be well compensated." Making my way out of the casino, I glanced over my shoulder; she was gone. Ryan might not like the ideas going through my mind, but it was the perfect solution. The only problem now would be putting my trust in a prostitute.

Back at the hotel, I turned on my phone and set it on the bed, ignoring its incessant beeping. It'd been a week since I'd talked to Ryan and the last thing I wanted was to hear him bitch. He was just going to have to go another day without talking to me. Running a hand through my hair, I looked out the window at the city lights. I prayed I could figure out the case before another woman went missing.

Over at the bar, a bottle of whiskey called my name. I was about to pour a tumbler full when a loud knock sounded on the door. *Who the fuck is that?*

As soon as I opened the door, the red-haired vixen strolled in, carrying a bag in her hands. "You decided to follow me? You should know I'm not into stalkers."

Throwing her bag on the floor, she turned to me, her smile gone. "It's a good thing I'm not stalking you then. My name's Aylee McFadden. I'm with the FBI." She lifted her leg on the couch and retrieved something strapped to her thigh, throwing it at me.

Eyes wide, I stared down at her badge. "Holy fuck."

CHAPTER 3

AYLEE

"I can't believe you were going to get a civilian to help you with the case, least of all a fucking prostitute," I scolded. Instead of answering, he clenched his jaw and tossed me my badge. "I'll give you credit though, at least you didn't try to fuck me."

He stepped forward, sliding his shirt sleeves up, showing off the tattoos tracing down his right arm; green eyes blazing. "My mind is always on the case. So what exactly does the FBI hope to accomplish by sending you?"

Reaching into my bag, I pulled out my detail assignment which now included him. "First off, I want you to stop talking to me like I'm the enemy." He scoffed, pissing me off more. "And second," I added, throwing the file at him, "it was my idea to risk my life to help *you*."

Hearing what was being done to the victims brought back horrible memories. I was sick for a week after looking at the pictures. I wasn't a weak woman, but there was only so much you could take before the past came back to haunt you. My eyes started to burn.

"So what, I'm supposed to take orders from you now?" he asked, breaking into my thoughts.

Rolling my eyes, I crossed my arms. "Is this really how you're going to be?"

He tossed the file on the couch. "I can do whatever the fuck I want. This is *my* case and I'm going to solve it. I don't need you or the bureau fucking everything up."

Barreling toward the door, I didn't even try to stop him. "Whiny bitch it is then," I muttered. Pulling out my phone, I dialed Ryan's number. He'd warned me about Jason's reaction.

"Let me guess, he told you to fuck off," he said, answering the phone.

"Not in those exact words, but I got the gist."

"He may be an arrogant jackass, but he's one of the best. I've been giving him hell the past month. It's never taken him this long to solve a case."

Sitting on the couch, I put the file on my lap and opened it. "That's because he can't do this one alone. He needs me, whether he likes it or not."

"Good luck with that. Make sure to keep me posted, he's been ignoring my calls."

"I will. All I have to do is get his considerable thick skull out of his ass."

Jason had been gone for hours and I wasn't about to wait up, so I went to bed. It was now morning and the bed was so warm, I didn't want to leave. It was almost as if the sheets were heated. Snuggling into them, I felt a puff of warm breath on my ear.

"What the flying fuck?" I screeched, elbowing the arrogant jackass behind me. I tried to get up, but Jason laughed, tightening his grip around my stomach. It wasn't the damn sheets keeping me warm, it was him.

"I think I like you better sleeping," he teased.

"Shut the hell up and let me go. What on God's green earth do you think you're doing?"

"We're lovers, sweetheart. Or at least that's what the file said. I was just getting into character."

I snorted and elbowed him again. "In *public*, asswipe. Behind closed doors, I want you to keep your grubby little carny hands off me."

Chuckling, he let me go and I rolled out of bed. Leaning on his elbow, he looked at me with a devilish smirk. "What happened there?" He pointed to my neck.

I quickly put my hand over the scar. "Mind your own business. If you're trying to run me off by being a dick, it's not going to work. I know who you are and what you're like, Mr. Avery. You like to work alone, I get that, but being an arrogant fool isn't going to help us solve the case. You need to work with me on this one."

"I am, or at least I'm trying to. We're supposed to be lovers. I don't see how that's going to work, considering you hate my guts."

I rolled my eyes. "If you read the complete file you'd see I'm actually going to be your companion. I fooled you earlier didn't I?"

He pursed his lips. "Don't you know how dangerous this is going to be? When we get on the inside, you'll be the target."

I shrugged. "That's the plan. I'm willing to put myself on the line for this."

"Why, because it's your job?" His piercing stare bore into mine.

"I have my reasons. Now can we get to work? We have a lot of ground to cover."

Throwing the covers off, he got out of bed stark ass naked. "Sure, but I should probably get dressed first."

Holy shit. Mouth gaping, I watched him walk out of the room. What had I gotten myself into?

CHAPTER 4

AYLEE

"Ariel, let's go," he called.

I finished the last touches of my makeup that ended up being about an inch thick and stuck my head out the bathroom door. "Are you seriously going to call me that?" When I got a good look at him, my breath caught. He was dressed in a suit with a pair of aviators hanging out the breast pocket. Why are all the hot guys such douchebags?

"If you don't like it you know where the door is." He smiled wide, daring me to leave.

"Nah, it's cool. I'll just call you Lester." I stepped back into the bathroom. "I'm not going anywhere, so you can stop trying to push me away."

"We'll see about that," he murmured low, probably thinking I couldn't hear him.

Sighing, I glanced at myself in the mirror. My hair was perfectly coifed and my black dress hugged my curves. Going undercover as a prostitute wasn't what I would've chosen on this case, but it was the only card I had to play. "Here goes nothing," I mumbled.

When I walked out, Jason's jaw clenched and instead of acknowledging me, he went straight for the door, opening it wide. He had both of our bags draped across his shoulder, and when I tried to grab mine, he gripped it tighter. Rolling my eyes, I strolled past him toward the elevator and pressed the button.

"Are you ready for this?" he asked.

I snorted. "I'm always ready. You?"

The elevator door opened and he followed me in, dropping our bags to the floor. Snaking his arm around my waist, he pulled me in close. I tried to stop from shivering and failed. He chuckled and slid his hand lower, but I knew what he was up to. Instead of removing his hand, I stood there, smirking.

"Very good, firecracker. I guess you are ready. Now what are you going to do if I do this?" He caged me in and backed me up against the wall, pressing his body into mine. His lips were so close I could feel his breath on my neck.

"I told you I'm fully dedicated to this case. I knew

what I was going to have to do with you. It's a small price to pay."

"And with the men we investigate . . . are you prepared to fuck them too?"

I narrowed my eyes. "I have my own agenda for them. And let's get this straight, I have no plans on fucking anyone while I'm here."

"Why not, you married?"

"No."

"Boyfriend?" he asked.

"Why do you want to know?"

He shrugged. "Don't want him trying to kick my ass after he finds out what we've done together."

"And what exactly is that?"

He smacked my ass and winked. "You'll see." The elevator doors opened and we stepped out into the lobby, his arm securely around my waist, with our bags hanging on his shoulder. A black limousine waited for us outside. Jason guided me toward the door as the driver opened it. "In you go." I slid in and he joined me, his thigh brushing mine. "Caesar's Palace," he commanded to the driver.

Jason pressed a button to lift the privacy window. "All right, let's quickly go over everything. Whatever you do, do *not* go anywhere out of my sight. I want to keep my eyes on you the entire time."

"Same goes for you. No horny waitresses, no corner

prostitutes, no escorts. I need to make sure you don't get distracted."

He chuckled. "Baby, I don't have to pay for sex. But now that I have you helping out, I might be able to squeeze in some fun time."

"By all means. Just make sure you go somewhere else and not in our room."

"Don't worry, I'm going to get us a suite with two rooms. That way we don't bother each other."

"As long as they have noise deadening walls, I'm good to go."

"So you're a screamer then?"

"What? I was talking about—" I shook my head. "Never mind."

His laugh made my teeth clench. "Looks like I made someone blush. I think it's kind of sexy."

I huffed. "All you've done is made my trigger finger twitchy. Keep it up and I'll be working this case alone."

The driver dropped us off at Caesar's Palace and before checking out the casino, Jason reserved us the penthouse suite. It was huge with two bedrooms, the epitome of luxury and elegance.

"You must've earned some serious money while you've been out here."

He chuckled. "You have no idea. Pick which room you want and I'll take the other. I made sure they were on opposite ends so you couldn't hear the screams of pleasure about to ensue. Wouldn't want you to get jealous."

"Jackass," I mumbled under my breath. "Doesn't matter much to me."

"And then once you're settled we'll have to work out a system."

"For what?"

"Like hanging a sock on the door knob when you're horny and looking for a little of this." He gestured down his body.

"Oh, good grief. That will never happen. Ever."

"Just remember . . . if you ask me to, I'm willing." He turned and walked away, shaking his butt before disappearing into the second bedroom.

As good looking as Jason was, I would never look at him that way. When working on a mission, it wasn't a good idea to get physically involved with a partner. That led to certain emotions and those types of feelings weren't good in life or death situations.

I walked into the first bedroom and set my bag down. I wasn't there to enjoy the scenery. Taking a deep breath, I walked out of the bedroom and straight to the bar. There was an assortment of liquors so I poured myself a vodka shot and downed it.

"Take it easy, killer. I don't want you getting too comfortable with the fellas tonight."

I snorted. "You have nothing to worry about. I've

seen pictures of the men we're investigating. The liquor is to help me see them in a new light."

"You did pretty well with me earlier," he noted. He stood in front of me as I poured another shot.

"It's all part of the job. Besides, I knew you."

"I see. So you think you know me, huh?"

"Well, maybe not really know you, but everyone in the field has heard your name. You have a reputation."

Pouring himself a shot of whiskey, he held the glass to his lips. "And what's said about me?" he asked, his eyes twinkling mischievously.

I tossed my shot back and cringed when it went down. "Stuff I'm sure you already know. You're a smooth talker, like breaking the rules, and a master manipulator. Not to mention you're a complete pain in the ass. I've also noticed you get angry when you don't get what you want. Some would call that temper tantrums."

"It looks like you have me all figured out. It's a shame I don't know much about you."

"Like you care anyway. I seem to recall you trying to get rid of me."

He winked. "I still am. You ready to go?"

I set my glass down and waved toward the door. "After you."

CHAPTER 5

JASON

I didn't want to be a dick, but dammit to hell, I was pissed. Even with all the work I'd done on the case, I knew without a doubt the FBI would take all the credit for solving it. The file was what really got me going. I didn't like people telling me what to do. It was my idea to hire Aylee in the first place, not knowing she was a fucking FBI agent. That was all me.

Seeing the way she handled my bullshit, there was no way I was going to be able to get rid of her. It was fun trying, even though I felt like a douche putting the moves on her when I knew she was only letting me touch her to prove a point. I couldn't deny the attraction I felt. Not only was she sexy as fuck, but she was strong and totally not interested. I had yet to meet anyone like her.

"Where do you want to start?" she asked, gazing around the casino.

Her body fit perfectly into my side as I held her close. "Have you ever been in a casino before?"

She shook her head. "I'm from Maine. The only casinos we have are in Oxford and Bangor. It's not exactly my cup of tea."

"I didn't know you were from Maine."

"That's because you've been too busy messing with me to ask. Have you ever been there?"

"No, but I've always wanted to visit the state. Unfortunately, nothing ever happens up there that needs my attention."

"Why do you think I live there? Okay, where do you want to start?" She glanced up at me, all business.

"Why don't *you* play tonight?"

Her eyes went wide. "Me? Are you insane? I don't know what the hell I'm doing."

Grabbing her hand, I pulled her with me and bought her a thousand dollars in chips. "It's easy. I'll show you what to do."

"I can't spend this," she gasped, refusing to take them. "I'll get my own."

I pushed them toward her and chuckled. "Tonight's on me. Let's just say it's an apology for being a dick."

"What if you're a dick tomorrow? Does that mean you'll give me two grand?"

I winked. "Only if you promise to win it back."

"What if I don't?"

I leaned down and whispered in her ear, placing my hands on her bare shoulders. "Then you'll owe me."

"Or," she murmured low, tilting her head to the side. "I can just kick your ass. What happens if I earn your money back and then some?"

"Then I'll stop fucking with you. But you're more than welcome to try and kick my ass. You'll have to do it in that dress though."

Snickering, she started toward the Blackjack table. "You are so gonna regret saying that."

"Oh yeah? How come?"

Looking back at me, she grinned wide. "You'll see."

Taking a seat at the table, she was up against two other men who couldn't stop making side glances at her. I wasn't the only one enamored. The best part was she didn't even notice the attention. She put her chips on the table and waited for the first card; it was a four of spades. I waited on her to ask me for guidance, but she didn't. She tapped the table for another card, and then another, smirking at me over her shoulder.

Kneeling down, I put my arm around her chair. "You dirty little liar. You know exactly what you're doing, don't you?" She won the match and pocketed an extra two hundred dollars.

"Of course, I do. I'd have been stupid not to. So stand back and watch how it's done. After tonight, you're going to get over yourself and work with me. Deal?"

She held out her hand. The girl was sly, I had to give her that. Her trick reminded me of something I'd do. Taking her hand, I pulled her to me. "Deal. But sooner or later you're going to play against *me*. Let's see how you do then."

CHAPTER 6

AYLEE

For the rest of the night, Jason watched me go from table to table, winning some and losing some. Luckily, I was able to earn over a thousand dollars. The only downside was that none of the men we'd been searching for visited the casino.

"Where do you think they are?" I asked, getting into the elevator. "These men are well-known. Surely, someone at these casinos knows them."

"I have no doubt, but we can't go around asking questions. We don't want anyone getting suspicious. It's not something we can risk right now."

"What about tailing them?"

The elevator door opened. "Tried that, didn't work.

I've even ridden by the ranch where the girls live. It's like the playboy mansion on steroids. I'm sure any woman would sell her body to live there. The only way you get in, is if you pay. And I'm not talking just a hundred dollars."

"How much?" I asked.

We got to our suite and walked in. "Five grand. You also get a sample of the product. I think I had a choice between a hand job or getting my dick sucked."

I scoffed. "Are you serious? How do you know this?"

He rolled his eyes. "I called and asked." Then he winked. "But don't worry, I have no desire to be with a woman who's had her mouth on ten thousand dicks."

I snorted. "A little hypocritical aren't we? I'm sure you've had your cock in a fair share of women."

Loosening his tie, he sat down on the couch, smirking. "You're right, I have, but a guy has to have some sort of standards. Besides, I think I'm starting to prefer the unattainable. I don't like having things handed to me." He gazed at me like I was an obstacle that needed to be conquered, but I didn't back down.

"Neither do I, but if you're referring to me you might as well get your jollies at the whorehouse, because you will never get any of this." I pointed to myself.

"Then I guess it's a shame the ranch isn't open for business."

"Thank God for that," I mumbled.

Turning on the television, Jason sat there with a smile on his face. I hated that he enjoyed tormenting me. What I really wanted to do was beat the shit out of him, but the last thing I needed was for him to know he could get under my skin. Instead of continuing the conversation, I started for my bedroom and slammed the door shut. I kicked off my high heels and peeled off the skin tight dress. I hated wearing dresses and I abhorred wearing a lot of makeup. Give me a pair of jeans and a T-shirt and I'd be happy.

After scrubbing the shit off my face, I hopped in the shower and sighed. My muscles were tense and loosened once the hot water ran over my skin. I don't know how long I stayed in there, but my fingers were shriveled prunes by the time I got out. There was no sound coming from the living room, so I dressed in a pair of pajama pants and a T-shirt before quietly opening my bedroom door. Once I saw the room was dark, I tiptoed to the kitchen and opened the refrigerator.

"You look different."

Gasping, I grabbed my chest and turned around. Jason flipped on the lights and grabbed an apple from the fruit bowl. "You scared the shit out of me," I hissed, reaching for a bottle of water and slamming the refrigerator closed.

"Sorry, I heard your footsteps."

"No, you didn't. You were being a creeper. There's no way in hell you heard me."

Chuckling, he sat down and patted the stool beside his. "You're right, I didn't. I couldn't sleep."

Now that my heart stopped racing, I sat down and watched him take a bite of his apple. "So I look different, huh? Good or bad?"

He chewed his apple, smiling wide. "Good. You're much prettier without all that shit on your face." Lifting his finger, he traced it over my cheeks. "Your freckles are cute."

"Cute?" I scoffed, slapping his hand away. "Do you have any idea how many times I hear that crap? It's annoying and makes me feel like a child."

"Believe me, you don't look like one. I wouldn't be wasting my time on you if you did."

"You're already wasting your time. The only action you're getting from me is a job well done. That's it."

He took another bite of his apple, smiling. "I'll take any *job* you're willing to give me. It's better than nothing."

The man was insufferable. "I take it you don't have a girlfriend waiting on you back home."

Tossing the rest of his apple into the trash, he wiped his hands on his shorts. "Nope. I'm too busy to date."

I understood that all too well. "Tell me about it. When I'm not away on missions, I help my uncle and his partner with their bed and breakfast. It's nice to get that time away with the stuff we do."

"Escape from what?" he asked, moving to the couch.

I followed him into the living room and sat in the chair across from him. "Do you even care to know?"

His smile faded. "You won the deal and I promised I'd get off your case about leaving. I never said I'd stop fucking with you. It's who I am and what I do. You just have to get over it. On the other hand, you're basically my partner. Your wellbeing depends on me and vice versa. I think it's time we establish some trust. I may joke about your hot pussy, but that doesn't mean I'm trying to get in it."

I blushed at the ease in which he said the word pussy. "Easier said than done. I've put my trust in other agents before and suffered the consequences. I know not to make that same mistake again."

"What happened?"

"It's not really something that's easy for me to talk about." I leaned over on my elbows and yawned.

He mimicked my movement and stared at me. "I get it. In a way, I think we've all been fucked over one way or another."

"What's your story?" I asked.

He shook his head. "You tell me yours and I'll tell you mine."

"Maybe someday. Right now, I'm going to bed."

Standing, I started for my room and then turned, his eyes following me. "And there's not going to be a sock on my door so don't even bother waiting for it."

He chuckled and got to his feet. "Sweet dreams, firecracker."

The next morning, I woke up earlier than Jason and ordered breakfast. I didn't want to wake him so I ate and studied the suspects' files. All of the men were wealthy business owners of sorts; powerful men. One of them was obviously paying off the media. After eating breakfast, I slipped on my bikini and slid my clothes over it. If Jason was going to sleep all day, I wanted to at least enjoy the free time to clear my mind. I could always think better outside. Grabbing the sunglasses out of my bag, I slid them on top of my head and wrote Jason a note saying I was at the pool.

By the time I got down there, it was still early enough to where there weren't that many people. I grabbed a water from the bar, took off my shirt and shorts, and laid out by the pool.

"Would you like a cocktail?"

I looked up at the waiter and smiled. "Oh dear God, no. It's too early for me to drink."

With a devilish grin, his white teeth stood out from

his tanned skin. "It's five o'clock somewhere, right?"

"True, but I'll pass. Maybe in a couple of hours."

"I'll be back later then. Enjoy your morning." He strolled off and started flirting with a couple of older women who just ate him up like a doughnut.

Sitting back in my chair I watched as gradually more people congregated around the pool. I loved to read, but people watching was always better. One thing the bureau loved about me was that I didn't look the part. I may be a red-haired and pale-skinned Irish girl, but I could kick some serious ass. Many people have gone up against me and failed miserably.

After a couple of hours of keeping to myself underneath the large umbrella, I spotted a group of young men with their plaid shorts and boat shoes. Frat boys by the looks of them. They sat across the pool from me, but I could see them staring. It wasn't long before one of them got up and walked over.

"Excuse me," he said.

I slid my glasses on top of my head. "What can I do for you?"

"Well, um, I have a question."

I had a feeling it was going to be one I didn't want to answer. "Okay, shoot."

He licked his lips and looked back at his friends who all waited on the edge of their seats. "My friends want to know if your hair is as red down there as it is on top of your head." The poor boy looked uncomfortable as hell and I was about to make it worse.

"Down where? I don't understand," I said, acting innocent.

Hesitating, I could see the sweat beading on his brow. It took all I had not to laugh and punch him at the same time. Moving a step closer, he sat down on the edge of the seat, turning his back to his friends. "Please just smack me and get it over with. It's part of my initiation."

"You *are* a frat boy. So tell me, what happens if I don't smack you?"

"I lose points."

"And you honestly think saying shit like this to women is worth it? What if I was your mother someone was doing this to?"

"Hey, honey," a voice called from behind me.

I turned around as Jason planted his lips on mine. He nipped my bottom lip, and I gasped. Pulling away, I saw he was dressed in a white T-shirt and khaki shorts, his tattoos showing through the fabric. The frat guy's face turned pale and he started to leave, but Jason grabbed him by the neck.

"Not so fast, shithead. What's this I hear about finding out the color to *what*?"

"It was just a joke," the guy whimpered.

"Just a joke my ass. Which one of your fucktard

friends put you up to this?"

"Th—the one in the pink and gray striped shorts."

Jason glared over at the guys and they all froze. It took all I had not to laugh. "What is it with you pansies wearing pink?"

I thought Jason would let him go, but instead, he tossed him into the pool and stalked straight over to the guys who tried to get away. They weren't fast enough. Jason grabbed the guy in the pink shorts – wedgie style – and lifted him in the air. The guy cried out while his friends stood there and laughed. Jason threw him as hard as he could into the pool and he belly flopped into the water.

Crossing my arms, I watched as Jason strolled back over to me with a million watt smile on his face. "That felt so damn good."

"I could've taken care of it myself."

Leaning down, he grabbed my water and handed it to me. "I have no doubt, but I came down here to get you. We have to go."

"Well, damn. I thought you were coming to hang out and get some sun."

He looked around at all the people at the pool. "I'd prefer not having people stare at me."

"Conceited much?" I mentioned, getting to my feet.

His smile faded. "If only it were that simple. Actually, Ryan called. Another girl's gone missing. He wants us at the station."

Nodding quickly, I threw on my T-shirt and shorts and was ready to go.

CHAPTER 7

AYLEE

"This one's different," I stated, looking down at the picture. It's a woman in her early-thirties who was celebrating a weekend with her girlfriends.

Ryan nodded. "Since she isn't a hooker, I don't know if we're looking for the same suspect or not. All her friends said she was meeting someone at the Bellagio. They don't know who or what he looks like. Phone calls aren't going through and until she's gone for a full twenty-four hours, there's nothing we can do."

"Do you want to go to the Bellagio tonight and take a look around?" Jason asked.

I nodded. "Maybe we'll finally have some luck tonight."

Closing the file, Ryan sat back in his chair. "It looks like you two are getting along better."

"Don't get too carried away. It's only because he lost a bet and his ego's sore," I said.

Ryan shrugged. "Either way, we need to get this shit figured out soon."

Jason regarded him, his expression serious. "We'll figure it out, Chief. Like you, we don't want to lose anyone else. It wouldn't be so bad if we could get close to the cocksuckers."

"I understand. But I have faith you will."

The way back to the hotel was silent. I could see the wheels in Jason's head turning. "What are you thinking about?"

Frustrated, he ran a hand through his hair. "Honestly, I feel like a goddamned failure. It's never taken me this long to solve a case. The longest has been a couple of weeks, tops."

"Don't be so hard on yourself. Not every case can be solved at the drop of a hat."

"What about you? What's your longest?"

"Three weeks. And it was the worst three weeks of my life."

"Why is that?"

Closing my eyes, the memories flashed, replaying like a vivid dream. "It was personal. The suspects had taken something away from me. And when I found them, I took something away from them." My eyes burned and I could feel the moisture welling behind my closed lids.

"What?" he asked.

Looking over at him, I couldn't stop the dreaded tear from falling down my cheek. "Their lives."

"I have a good feeling about tonight," Jason insisted.

He hadn't mentioned anything about what we talked about on the ride home, and I was very grateful. I needed to make sure my head was in the game and not in that dark place. "Good. Maybe that means we'll find the bastards we're looking for."

"We will," he said, his reflection appearing in the mirror. He looked at me, his lips tilting up into a lazy smile. "You look beautiful."

I glanced at myself in the mirror. "Flattery will get you nowhere, Avery."

He shrugged. "Just speaking the truth."

"No sense on wasting your game when no one here cares for it."

"Can you honestly not accept a compliment?"

"Not from you."

"I can't believe you don't like my southern charm." He looked completely bewildered.

"The ladies love that shit, even if they're stuck-up Yankees."

I let out a dry laugh. "I've lived in the south too, numbskull. My father was in the Navy so we traveled a lot."

"Now we're getting somewhere. I thought I could hear a bit of twang in there. Do you have any brothers or sisters?"

Sighing, I took a final look at myself in the mirror and turned around. "No, it was just my mom, dad, and me." I walked past him to the kitchen and kept my back to him while I poured a shot of his whiskey, tossing it back quickly.

"Do they live in Maine too?"

Clenching my teeth, I poured another shot. "What's with all the questions?" I glanced at him over my shoulder.

With narrowed eyes, he studied me. "I'm good at reading people, but I can't seem to figure you out." Sliding his laptop over, he opened it and typed away. "With just a touch of a few keys, I can find out anything I want about someone. You? I can't find shit."

I turned around, hands on my hips. "So you've been investigating me, why?"

He closed his laptop. "I worked with a guy for years who fucked over my entire team without us knowing. That's how good he was. He wanted someone on the inside of the government so he could help his brother with all sorts of illegal shit. Not to mention, the fucker almost killed my sister in his quest for revenge. Trust is a big issue with me."

"It is with me too. Do you not think I am who I say I am?"

"I don't know. All I could find was an article with you and your uncle at his bed and breakfast and that you graduated from George Washington University. It's like you're a ghost."

"Obviously not everything was taken away if you were able to find that." I stalked over to him, eyes blazing. "But if you want to know the truth, I'll tell you. You should be able to recognize if I've been lying or not. It's one of the first things we learned."

"You're right, but the problem is, *you* haven't told me a fucking thing about yourself. I have nothing to go on, no base for my trust."

"Fine." I twisted the seat beside him and sat, knees to knees with my hands palms up in his lap. "I'll tell you whatever you want to know."

The second he touched my wrists, my pulse spiked. "Nervous?"

I kept my focus on his eyes, knowing I couldn't lie. "Yes, but only because I'm not used to being touched."

"Do you think I'm sexy?" he asked, winking.

I jerked out of his hold, glaring. "I didn't offer to do

this so you could provoke me. Just ask your questions so we can get to work."

He grabbed my wrists and put his thumbs back in place. "Is your name Aylee McFadden?"

"Yes."

"Are you really an FBI agent?"

"Yes."

"Why is your profile untraceable?"

I sighed. "Because I don't want to be found."

"Why?"

"There was a time many years ago when someone tried to find me to get to my dad. They ended up finding my mother instead."

"What happened?" he asked, sounding concerned.

"I don't want to talk about it."

"Either you talk about it with me now, or I will find it myself. I don't think you want me picking apart your life."

His threat was not a bluff because I could see it in his eyes. "My father was big into gambling. I didn't know until later that we moved around a lot because he'd made enemies. One night, he lost big and didn't have the money to pay. Before he could get us out of town, the men came . . ." My voice cracked and took a deep breath, blowing it out slowly.

"My father was able to get me out of the house unseen and he told me to run, so I did. They were coming for me as payment. It wasn't until I was working for the bureau that I saw what they did to them. My uncle lied to me and said they were shot, but that wasn't the case. They raped my mother in front of my father and then beat her to death. The men left, leaving my father alive, but he ended up taking his own life before the cops arrived."

Tears fell down my cheeks and Jason let go of my wrists so he could wipe them off. I flinched at the contact. "I'm sorry, Aylee."

"Not many people know. I don't ever talk about it. At the time, I was living in Florida, but then moved to Maine to be with my uncle and his boyfriend. Now they're married. When I got older, I went to school and was lucky enough to get where I am today."

"Did the police ever catch the men who killed your parents?"

I shook my head. "I did. I got good at tracking people and I found them."

Instead of checking my pulse, he caressed his thumbs soothingly across my wrists. "Then what did you do?"

"I killed both of them. It took three miserable weeks of being undercover and when one of them attacked me, I put a bullet in his head."

"Were you there alone or did you have a partner?"

My jaw clenched. "I had one. He betrayed me for fifty thousand dollars and told them who I was. Too bad he never got the money. Once they had me in their grasp, they killed him, but not before he was able to wound the other guy. If he hadn't done that, I don't know if I'd be here right now." I lowered my head.

"I think your trust issues are warranted."

I wiped my eyes. "Being untraceable helps me feel safe. That's why I changed to my mother's maiden name, McFadden."

"Are you Irish?"

I nodded. "My mother's side. She was going to take me to Ireland, but never got the chance. I have my uncle though. He's all the family I ever needed." Sliding out of the chair, he let me go so I could walk into the living room. "Are we done with the questions?"

"Not unless you want to ask me some," he countered.

I glanced back at him. "I already know everything about you, remember?"

He chuckled. "Maybe, but I'm sure there's a lot you don't."

His statement was true, but we didn't have the time. "You're right, but it's getting late. I just hope I've earned a little bit of your trust."

He put his hand on my shoulder and turned me around. "You have, but I have yet to earn yours."

I shrugged. "It doesn't matter. I learned to take care of myself a long time ago." Stalking past him, I picked up my clutch and stood by the door. "Ready?"

He joined me and slid on his black blazer. "One

way or another, I will earn your trust. Even if you don't believe me, I do take this job seriously. I won't fail you like your last partner."

We'll see about that.

CHAPTER 8

AYLEE

It was Saturday night and the Bellagio was packed. The strip really came alive at night. Vegas was indeed the city that never slept. Putting his hand on my waist and sliding it down, Jason leaned toward my ear. "Do you want to play tonight?" he asked, squeezing one of my butt cheeks in his palm.

I shook my head and smiled, speaking through clenched teeth. "After I break your hand, I might."

Laughing, he moved his hand away. "Just keeping you on your toes, firecracker."

"More like setting yourself up for harassment charges. I think I'm just going to follow you around. If we do find who we're looking for, I need to look like arm candy — not a woman who could obviously dominate you."

He held out his arm. "Let's go then, before you turn me on any further."

Rolling my eyes, I took his arm and we set off to get chips. When he asked for ten thousand dollars worth, I almost fell to the floor. "Holy crap," I whispered, holding his arm tight. "Are you going to spend all of that?"

Chuckling, he patted my hand. "You've got to spend big to win big. But don't worry, I expect to double up. All we have to do now is get in the door."

I looked around the casino and so far no one of importance had popped up. "Where are we going first?"

"Poker tables, baby. That's where the money is."

We set off toward the tables and he sat down while I stood back, watching. My father had taught me how to play poker, especially Texas Hold'em. It was my favorite game as a kid. A part of me wanted to join in on the fun, but I had a part to play. Jason glanced back at me and I pointed to the tables off to the side; he nodded and winked.

As soon as I sat down, one of the waitresses came over. She had short black hair and a face for magazines. "Would you like something to drink?"

"A raspberry martini would be great, please."

"Of course. Anything else?"

"No, that will be all. But say, it seems kind of dead in here. Is it always this slow?"

She shook her head. "The high rollers usually show up around ten o'clock. I have to be on my game when they do. They tip the best."

"I can imagine." As soon as she sauntered off, I checked the time on my phone. It was nine-thirty. I needed to be on the lookout if what she said was true. The waitress came back with my martini so I sipped on it lightly while I watched Jason's game from afar.

It wasn't long before a man walked in, surrounded by two men and a woman on his arm. I could feel the power rolling off him in waves. He wasn't one of the suspects on our list, but I had no doubt he could lead us to them. He was middle-aged and so was the woman. From the wedding band on her finger, I assumed she wasn't a prostitute.

The next time Jason looked back at me, I nodded toward the group. Keeping my eyes on the target, I watched them as they walked through the casino, speaking to people in passing.

"What's going on?" Jason asked, brushing up against me.

I jumped, not expecting him to be done so fast. "What the . . . why did you leave the table?"

He shrugged. "This is more important. I only lost two hundred anyway."

"Thank goodness it wasn't the ten grand. You might need it."

Jason followed my gaze. "I wonder who that is."

"I don't know, but we need to find out. I say we test the waters a bit."

A mischievous gleam twinkled in his eyes. "And it looks like they need more players. Come on," he said, taking my hand. We walked casually toward the table and there were still two spots left. "Wish me luck." He placed a kiss on my cheek, his stubble brushing against my skin.

"Good luck," I stuttered as he walked off, taking a seat at the table. So far so good.

"Isn't he just sex on a stick?" a voice called out from behind.

More like a pain in the ass. I turned to see the woman who walked in with the men. Her blonde hair was pulled high into an elegant updo and being the age she was, she looked amazingly fit in her tight green dress and tan skin.

"Are you two married?" she asked, looking down at my hand.

Putting on a fake smile, I shook my head. "No, we're not."

"Engaged?"

I chuckled. "No, nothing like that."

Her eyes went wide. "Oh, I think I get it now. I apologize. You'd think I'd be used to it by now. These men are always looking for a good time. You're not one of Chatfield's girls are you?"

I shook my head. "I'm on my own. She doesn't seem to be taking on any new talent at the moment."

She pursed her lips. "I think it's because some of her girls went missing. I'm not sure what's going on though because I still see some of them around William's friends. All I can say is it's a dangerous job. You never know what kind of bloke you're going to end up with."

"Trust me, I've met my fair share of interesting men." Jason, of course, was one of them. Clearing my throat, I pointed to the table. "I assume you're married to one of them over there?" I asked.

She nodded. "Going on thirty years now. He's the one with the white hair, wearing the blue shirt," she said, pointing at the man I hoped Jason could get close to. The other two were younger and more military looking. "No matter how many whores, excuse the word, sweetheart, try to get close to him, he's never let me down. His friends, on the other hand, I can't say much for."

"I would hope he'd stay faithful to you. You're stunning," I admired, glancing up and down her body. "Not many women can maintain that kind of look."

Her smile widened and she held out her hand. "I

think I'm going to like you. My name's Diane Randall."

I took her hand. "Aylee McFadden."

"Well, Aylee, I think we need to get a round of drinks."

CHAPTER 9

JASON

The pot was five thousand dollars and six of the men had already abandoned the game. It was now between me and the three men Aylee and I were watching. The time had come for the river card which happened to be the last round of dealing. With the cards on the table and the two I had in my hand, I had a full house. The only plays that could beat me would be a four of a kind, straight flush, or a royal flush. The chances of the latter two were slim.

"Check," the older man with the white hair said. He stared at me with a hint of arrogance but also curiosity. The man had to be pushing sixty years old. The other men followed suit and checked. Now it was up to me. If

I checked, that meant no one had to pay money for that round. But if I put money in, they had to in order to stay in the game.

It just so happened I was in the mood to take chances. "All in," I announced, sliding eight grand into the middle of the table.

"Fold," the big, burly guy said. From the looks of him, I'd say he was security detail. He had that air about him with his oversized muscles and shaved head, most likely ex-military. The other guy looked the same way. It only peaked my interest in finding out who the man in the blue shirt was. Once the other big guy folded, it was down to me and Mr. Blue.

Smiling wide, he pushed his chips into the pot. "Call." He turned over his cards and showed the table his flush of hearts. The men with him grinned and waited for me.

"Good hand, but not good enough." I flopped my cards down and smiled wide.

The man in the blue shirt bellowed out a laugh and clapped his hands. "Fantastic! What's your name, my boy?"

We stood and I shook his hand. "Jason Avery."

"Well, Mr. Avery, I'm Will Randall. And these two," he said, waving his hand at his mammoth friends, "are my bodyguards, Butch and Tom. I don't think I've seen you here before."

Butch and Tom held out their hands so I shook them. "Good to meet you." Then to Will I said, "No, you most likely haven't seen me. I moved here about three months ago. So far, I'm enjoying it."

He chuckled. "From what I've seen, I'd say so. What exactly do you do?"

I glanced around the casino, grinning. "I left an accounting job in Chicago and came here to try my luck. I was sick of sitting behind a desk. But I have to say Sin City's been good to me."

"It's been good to me too," he replied.

"So what do you do that would require bodyguards? You must be an important man."

He chuckled. "I'm the CEO and owner of Randall Industries. I deal with real estate development, entertainment, music, you name it. I wear many hats."

"Sounds interesting."

"Oh, it is, or I wouldn't be doing it." Glancing over his shoulder, he found Aylee and the other woman sitting on one of the plush sofas, drinking. "Let's say we join our women for drinks before starting another game? You up for that?"

"You're on."

He slapped me on the back. "And then tomorrow, you can come back and we'll do it all over again."

"Sounds even better."

"I think the night was very productive," Aylee claimed. "After talking to Diane, I seriously think we need to find Madame Chatfield and have a chat with her. Do you know where she lives?"

As a matter of fact, I did. "We can check out her place tomorrow and see if she leaves. The last time I followed her, she ended up going to a fucking toy store. And I'm not talking Toys R Us."

Aylee laughed. "I had you pegged wrong, Avery. I thought you'd be into the butt plugs."

"Butt plugs, no. But I'm open to almost anything." I skimmed my finger across her neck. "I bet you have a secret collection of giant cocks stashed away somewhere."

"If I don't have time for the real thing, what makes you think I'd have it for the fake ones?" she grumbled.

I shrugged. "I'm a guy. It's fun to imagine."

"Okay, moving on. What do you think about Will? His wife was really nice. I didn't get any bad vibes from her." Back to business as usual with her stubborn brow.

"And I didn't get any from Randall," I said, agreeing with her. We had hoped Will would elaborate on who his friends were, but he didn't. "Are you looking up information on him?" I asked, glancing over at her across the room.

She was sitting in the large, brown leather chair in the corner with her laptop on her thighs. "How did you guess?"

"Because I'm doing it too. Let me know what you find." I stared at her profile, enjoying the way she concentrated on the screen, her bottom lip being pulled between her teeth. Once we'd gotten back, she'd changed out of her dress and put on a pair of shorts and tank top with her hair pulled high in a ponytail. She was sexy in her dress, but nothing could beat how fucking hot she was now; it was distracting.

Her gaze lifted and strayed over my way and I couldn't help but smile at how I made her shiver. "You're welcome for tonight," she stated, jutting her chin in the air.

"For what?"

"For being vigilant. If it wasn't for me, you wouldn't have seen Will or his people."

I snorted. "I would've seen them eventually. I can't help it you were drooling over Butch and Tom."

"Fuck that," she exclaimed, throwing a couch pillow at my head. I ducked behind my screen and laughed. "Why can't you tell me thank you?"

I reached for the pillow and threw it back at her. "Stop gloating and I will," I backfired. She made a face, thinking I couldn't see it. "You sure do have a temper to go with that red hair, don't you?"

"Only when I'm around you."

Shaking my head, I smiled; I liked her fiery temper. If only I could get her to loosen up a bit. The chances of that were slim to none. From the information on the computer, Will Randall was basically a celebrity in Vegas. "I got a lot coming up on Randall," I said.

She got up and sat beside me on the couch. "So have I. I did a search on Google and about a gazillion links popped up. It said his company is one of the biggest in the world."

"I see that." He was probably one of the richest men I'd ever met. "Do me a favor and look up stuff on his wife and family? I'm going to look at his company. He said he dabbled in a lot of things. I wonder if fucking hookers is a part of his daily regimen."

Aylee shook her head. "I don't think so. Diane said his friends frequently partake, but that he doesn't. She was pretty certain."

I snorted. "It's possible, but it wouldn't surprise me if a guy like Randall didn't have him some side-pussy. Men like that cheat, sweetheart."

She turned her computer my way. "You don't know that. He looks happy with his family in these pictures." I looked over to see him smiling with his wife and two daughters. Anyone could smile for the camera. "His wife also has a charity that helps autistic kids. It's dedicated to one of their daughters. On the outside, they look like good people."

"You and I both know that doesn't mean shit."

She sighed. "I know, and it's disheartening. Diane and Will actually seem like good people. I enjoyed talking to them tonight."

I did too, which was shocking. The more time we spent with him, the more I'd get an idea of his character. Aylee closed her laptop and set it on the coffee table before heading into the kitchen. She shuffled around and then the smell of popcorn wafted through the air.

"What are you doing?"

"I'm hungry. I saw a box of popcorn in here earlier."

"You gonna share?" I asked.

"Depends."

"On what?"

She didn't answer, choosing to focus on her task. Once the popcorn was done, she poured it into a bowl and sat down beside me, being a tease. I tried to grab a handful but she smacked my hand. I had a feeling she was waiting to hear something from me first. "Please," I begged, leaning in to get a better whiff.

She shook her head and stuffed her mouth full. "Nope."

I bit my lip and watched her lick the salt off her fingers. Holy fuck she was killing me. "Do you have any idea how sexy you are?"

Eyes wide, she choked on her popcorn and coughed, gasping for air.

I patted her on the back, trying to contain my laugh. "You all right?"

"Yeah, I just wasn't expecting you to say that."

Keeping my gaze on hers, I grabbed a handful of popcorn. "I'm not always an arrogant jackass, Aylee. With that being said, thank you for being vigilant tonight. I know that's what you wanted to hear."

"Do you mean it?" she asked.

Smiling wide, I tossed the popcorn in mouth. "We might end up being a good team after all." The problem was, I was beginning to want more.

CHAPTER 10

AYLEE

"So far so good," I said, stretching my calves. Jason's voice was in my ear as I ran in circles up and down the street in front of Madame Chatfield's estate. She lived behind a large, wrought iron gate in a mansion three times the size of my uncle's bed and breakfast.

"You doing okay? Not tired yet?"

I knew he could see me, but I couldn't see him. "I'm fine. Just hoping I'm not running around like this for nothing."

"Your effort is not going unnoticed. You should wear those shorts more often."

Lifting my hand, I fixed my ponytail and flipped

him off.

He chuckled. "I saw that."

"Good. Time for lap four." Taking a deep breath, I let it out slowly and picked up my feet. I was in really good shape, but the Vegas heat was torture. Maine was much more pleasant. Lifting my shirt, I used it to wipe the sweat off my forehead; it was already burning my eyes.

"Stop, firecracker. The gate just opened. Be ready to get in the car."

Leaning over on my knees, I caught my breath. "Ten-four." It wasn't long before his silver Nissan GT-R sped around the corner. I hopped in as fast as I could and buckled up. "You haven't lost her, have you?"

"Nope, we'll catch up." Turning the car around, he sped off in the direction he just came.

"Are you sure it was her in the car?"

"Positive. I don't think any of the escorts have white hair and wrinkles."

"Never know. Chatfield might be exploring the possibilities of granny porn."

Jason shivered. "Fuck that."

We finally caught up to Chatfield and followed her down to the strip. "Where do you think she's going?"

"Don't know, but put this on," he said, tossing a baseball hat onto my lap. "We don't want her being able to recognize us."

I put it on and tucked my hair underneath, making sure my sunglasses were in place. Once we got to the section of hotels, her car turned into Caesar's and stopped at the entrance. She got out and headed inside while her car stayed in the front. "What are we going to do?"

Parking quickly, he grabbed his gun out of the center dash and holstered it under his shirt. "We're going to take her for a ride."

Securing the hat on my head, I turned to him. "Let's go."

Putting on a pair of sunglasses and a hat as well, Jason smiled and got out of the car. Chatfield's chauffeur sat in the driver's seat with the window down. He was an elderly man, probably in his mid-sixties. Hopefully, we wouldn't give him a heart attack.

"What if she's a part of what's going on? This could blow our whole cover," I said, rushing across the parking lot.

"It could, but I'm hoping with her being out of business it's a good sign. We have to take risks. When I get in, hop in the back and be prepared. As soon as she gets in the car, I'll get us moving."

"Got it."

We approached the car and the driver looked up. Jason flashed his badge and opened the door. "If you don't mind, sir, I need you to move over, *now*."

The driver held up his hands and moved over, his voice shaking. "Is something wrong, officer?"

"I just want to talk to Madame Chatfield." Nodding at me, I got in and the driver turned a weary brow my way. "Please don't hurt my lady." He was genuinely scared.

"We just want to talk to her," I assured him.

"She's been so upset with everything going on. I don't want her stressed any more than she already is."

Jason snorted. "Take it easy. We're the good guys here."

The man still stared wearily at us. Luckily, we didn't have to wait long for Madame Ronnie Chatfield to waltz out of the hotel. I moved over to the far corner of the limo so she couldn't see me until after she got in. Before the driver could heed a warning, I jumped up and slammed the door shut, just as Jason took off.

Gasping, Ronnie clutched her chest, dropping her bag on the floor. "What the hell is the meaning of this? Who are you?" To be the owner of a well-known whorehouse, you wouldn't suspect it by the way she looked. She was older with long, white hair, dressed in a chic pantsuit, and no doubt the product of extensive plastic surgeries. I guess she could afford it having over a hundred women and men under her belt.

"We're just here to ask you a few questions. If there's nothing to hide, there won't be a problem. I'm with the

FBI."

Her gaze narrowed. "How do I know that?"

I quickly flipped out my badge, putting my thumb over my picture and name. "Believe me now?"

She sighed and sat back. "What can I do for you? I already told the police everything I know."

"Yes, but you failed to give them the names of your johns."

Swallowing hard, she choked back a sob. "Believe me, I would if I could. The kind of men I deal with aren't just your run of the mill crowd. They're powerful. They would run me into the ground and take everything I have. The deals we make are basically written in blood. I can't verbally tell you the information."

"But someone's killing your girls. Doesn't that make you want to do something about it?"

Her eyes blazed. "I *am* doing something about it. I shut down my business so none of them could get hurt. No matter what I've done, it hasn't helped. My girls are still disappearing."

"Are they accepting contracts without your knowledge?"

"That's what I'm assuming. Some of my girls don't mind the added risk. They want the money. I saw on the news about that young girl from Vermont who was reported missing yesterday. Do you think she's another victim?"

"We don't know," Jason spoke up. "From her stats, she doesn't exactly fit the hooker profile. She's an elementary school teacher here to have some fun with her friends. The killer doesn't seem to want that type, but I could be wrong. It'd be good to have some names."

She huffed. "I told you, I can't verbally tell you. What part of that do you not understand?"

I studied her and then caught onto her clue. "Great, then I will just list off the names we have and all you have to do is nod when you hear one who fits the bill."

A small smile splayed across her face. "Good catch, detective. Trust me, I want to see my girls safe again. I'll do anything I can to help, but I have to play by the rules."

"You're killing me, smalls," Jason grumbled from the front. "I never would've thought you'd be smarter than me."

Ronnie snorted. "She's a female. Of course she's smarter than you."

I held back my laugh; especially when Jason cursed to himself.

"I'm heading back to the hotel. Let's wrap this up," he ordered.

Clearing my throat, I looked straight at Ronnie, even though she couldn't see my eyes through the sunglasses. "I have a list of men we're investigating. I'm going to say their names and all you have to do is give me a simple nod. Ready?" She nodded. "Drake Blackwell?" She blinked and reluctantly nodded. "Mark Chamberlain?" Again, she nodded. "Chazz Davies?" Lowering her head, she nodded. "I have one more . . . Will Randall."

Chuckling, she leaned her head on the seat. "Oh, dear Lord, no. William isn't like the scumbags he hires. He's the last person I'd loan one of my girls out to. Believe me, they've asked, but he always refuses. If he didn't, I'd castrate him."

"Why is that?"

"We're family. His wife is my sister."

"I didn't see that coming, did you?" I asked.

Shaking his head, Jason pressed the button for our floor. We didn't want Madame Chatfield knowing we were staying at Caesar's so we'd waited for her to leave before venturing inside. "At least it clarifies that Randall hasn't been with any of the murdered girls. Unfortunately, he's still friends with our suspects. That could make him guilty by association. We can't trust any of these people."

"I wasn't planning on it. Hopefully, some of them will be at the casino tonight. I'm ready to get this shit over with." I looked at my watch. "What time do you want to head down to the casino to meet Randall?"

Jason set his phone on the counter when we got inside. "Probably around ten." Nodding, I started off toward my room. "Hey," he called.

Stopping, I slid my hair out of my ponytail and turned around, running my hands through it. "Yeah?"

His emerald eyes met mine and he had the cutest smirk on his face. "I was thinking, maybe we could get some dinner before work tonight? There's a restaurant in town and I kind of know the owners, or at least the owner's husband. I'm sure they'd reserve us a good table."

Hands on my hips, I studied him. "I'm not going on a date with you, Avery."

He chuckled and lifted his hands in the air. "It's a good thing it's not a date then. I thought I'd be polite and ask you to join me. But if you don't want to go . . ."

"No, I'll go," I blurted, maybe a little too excitedly. I cleared my throat and started again. "It'd be good to get something to eat. I don't want to go out by myself."

"Ah, so you're going with me because you don't want to be alone. I can't believe I finally found a girl who could actually resist me."

"Are you trying to tell me you can get any girl you want?" I asked incredulously. By the charming looks and devilish smile, I could believe it. I spent my whole life hating guys like him.

He shrugged. "Almost ninety-nine percent of the

time. Do you think I couldn't get you if I tried?"

"Oh, I know you can't, smart ass."

Smiling mischievously, his gaze never wavered from mine. "You're going to regret saying that, sweetheart. I might just have to prove you wrong."

I turned my back on him and walked to my room. "Whatever, Avery. I can't stop you from trying. I'll just be the one laughing and pointing when you fail."

CHAPTER 11

AYLEE

Why was it so difficult to read men like Jason? In the line of work he was pleasant and serious, but when it came to women he was arrogant, self-assured, and overly confident. I wanted to smack the smug from his face, or at least take him down a peg or two.

Taking a deep breath, I opened the door and stepped out. Jason looked over his shoulder and turned around, a glass of wine in his hands. He was dressed in a white collared shirt with the sleeves rolled up, showing his tattoos. "Looking sexy like always," he murmured, handing me the wine.

"Thank you. I didn't know we had wine."

He smiled. "I had it brought up." I took a sip of

the cool, crisp Riesling. "You really do look beautiful. I think green's your color."

"You think so?" I spun and stuck out my hip.

He smirked. "Hell yes. We make a hot pair."

I drank the rest of my wine and set it down on the counter. Biting my lip, I walked over to him, bringing my fingers up to his jawline. "We do, don't we?" I let my hand trail down his chest. "Say, what time is our ride going to be here?"

Jason's eyes got dark and he pulled me close. "I've got a ride for you right here," he rolled his hips into mine, "if you want to hop on."

"Seriously? Ew!" I smacked his arm and stepped back. "I was just teasing, and you—"

His laughter cut my words short. I watched as he shook his head and chuckled. "Like I didn't know what you were doing, sauntering across the room." He reached for his jacket and slipped it on. "You should have seen your face!"

"Ha-ha. Really funny, asshole." I rolled my eyes and huffed.

"Don't try to play a player, firecracker. Besides, if I was really trying . . . you'd be so caught up, you wouldn't even know it was happening."

I pouted. I hated being out-maneuvered.

"By the way, while you were getting dressed, I called and talked to Kacey. She's the owner of that restaurant

I told you about."

"Yeah? We get a table reserved?"

He winked, holding out his arm. "We have a lot more than that. Come on."

Taking his arm, he held it tight as we walked out the door to the elevator. My heels were a little taller tonight which made us almost the same height. Hopefully, I didn't fall flat on my face. The second I got home I was going to throw every single high heel into the garbage. Wearing them was torture, and unfortunately, I was thankful to have Jason to lean on.

"First day on heels?" he joked as I tried to get in the car.

"Hey, I can't help that your car's so low to the ground. Not to mention, I'm in a short ass dress. I don't want to show my lady bits to the whole world."

He froze as I got in the car. "You're not wearing any underwear?"

I winked up at him. "You'll never know."

He groaned. "You're going to fucking kill me." Then he shut the door and I laughed.

Yes, I was wearing underwear; I just liked torturing him. But after his moves back in the hotel room, I should probably have on a metal chastity belt like Marion in *Robin Hood: Men in Tights*.

Once on the road, the traffic was bumper to bumper. "It's just down the street," he informed me.

"How do you know the owner?"

"We're more like acquaintances really. The owner's husband is Tyler Rushing, the UFC Heavyweight Champion." He looked at me and I shook my head. I never kept up with MMA fighting to know who was who. "Anyway, I did some undercover work for a girl who works at his gym not too long ago. It's like a huge circle of friends."

He found a vacant parking spot and helped me out of the car, pulling my arm through his. I was going to tell him he didn't need to pretend, but I kind of liked being close to him. "I never really had a lot of friends; especially since my family moved around a lot. I guess you could say I've been kind of a loner. When I moved to Maine and things became more permanent, I was able to make friends. And by friends, I mean two."

"Three," he added. I lifted my brows and he winked. "Don't deny it. You're going to miss me when this case is solved."

"That's what you think," I countered.

When we got inside, Jason stood close to me, chills cascading down my skin. The host was a young man, probably in his early twenties. "Good evening. Do you have a reservation?"

"Yes, sir. It should be under Avery," Jason replied.

Nodding, the young man grabbed two fancy menus and led us past the tables to a circular staircase leading to the loft. There was just one table with candles and a bottle of wine. "This is for you," he said.

"Wow," was all I could muster.

Jason nudged me forward and pulled out my seat. "Aylee?"

"Oh," I laughed, snapping to attention. "This is all so . . ." I was thinking romantic but I didn't want to say it out loud.

"Mrs. Rushing said it had to be the best for her friends. I'm sure she'll be up here to greet you soon. Your waitress will be here shortly, would you like me to open the wine while you wait?"

Jason shook his head and sat down. "Nah, it's okay. I got it." Once alone, Jason opened the bottle and poured me a glass.

Taking the offered glass, I sipped the wine and swished it around my mouth; I was a wine whore. My uncle would always let me sample them when I was younger. When I got older, it was my job to pick out the types of wine we kept stocked for the guests. "I've never been out to dinner like this," I confessed.

He stared at me in disbelief. "You expect me to believe that?"

I shrugged. "Why not? It's the truth."

"I guess because someone like you has to have a million guys following you around. Didn't you date at all? What was your last boyfriend like?"

My lips turned up in a smile. "He was a good one, but not the kind of guy who was ready for a woman like me."

"How so? By the smile on your face, I'd say you still care for him," he mentioned, regarding me with serious eyes.

"He was one of my two friends. After we split up, I dated here and there, but nothing ever serious. Then when I got done with FBI training, I went back to Maine and we started a relationship again."

"Recent?" he asked.

"Not really. Things went downhill when I found out the truth about my parents. I was consumed with exacting revenge, while Adrian wanted to settle down with a wife and kids. I just couldn't commit."

"I'm sure you will one day. When that time comes, are you going back to him?"

Shrugging, I took another sip of wine. "I don't know. I'm not promised to live through this mission. I can't have kids and do this job. When I do decide to settle down, I'm not really sure where I want to be."

About that time, the waitress came up and I quickly looked through the menu and decided on the filet, Oscar-styled with au gratin potatoes. My stomach growled and Jason chuckled before ordering his food. When she left, his piercing green gaze bore into mine.

"So, basically what you're trying to say is that you

need adventure, someone who can keep up with you and not put a limit on what you can do."

I smiled. "Something like that. Why, you want the job?"

"I don't do long-distance, firecracker. Maine's a little far away from North Carolina."

"How will I ever find the strength to go on?" I asked. "Anyway, I bet you have tons of women waiting on you when you get home."

"Does that bother you?" he asked in all seriousness.

"Why would it?"

He poured himself a glass of wine and held it up. "Here's to our freedom." I touched my glass to his and we both took a sip.

We got back to Caesar's Palace around eight o'clock. Randall and his friends hadn't shown up yet so I decided to play my luck at the tables.

"Do you want some of my chips?" Jason asked.

Smiling, I shook my head. "Nope. I got this."

I paid for my own and walked to one of the Texas Hold'em tables. It was my favorite style of poker. There were a few men at the table, so I sat down and grinned. They looked at me like I was easy prey. Jason took the last seat.

"What are you doing? You're not supposed to play against me," I whispered low.

He smirked. "I couldn't resist. Let's see what you got."

The dealer passed out our cards and I gently lifted the corners to see what I had. *Not bad.* I had a queen of spades and a six of hearts. Jason winked at me and I rolled my eyes. Two of the men folded, which brought us down to seven players. The dealer laid out the flop which happened to be a two of diamonds, four of clubs, and a six of diamonds. A pair of sixes wasn't the best hand, but it was still something. Having my queen helped. The bid started out at a hundred dollars and Jason raised to two hundred. Keeping a straight face, I tossed in two hundred.

Jason's gaze focused on something across the room and he tensed, knocking my knee with his. "Incoming," he warned.

I looked over to see Will walk in with a group of men in tow, which seemed to be made up of the entire pool of suspects we were investigating, minus Drake Blackwell. Will found us and directed his friends to another table before coming to ours.

"Good evening, Mr. Randall," the dealer announced.

"Same to you, my friend." The energy in the room lifted and the men all sitting at our table sat straighter, puffing out their chests. It was funny how people liked to be intimidating. Will didn't seem to be effected at all. Instead, he watched the game in amusement.

After the last card was thrown down by the dealer, everyone checked except Jason, who tossed in three hundred more. Knowing he was either bluffing or just lucky, I called, determined not to back down. Four of the other players folded, leaving one other player in the game. Turning over his cards, he revealed a pair of fours. Judging by the look on his face, he knew he was grasping for straws.

"What ya got, firecracker?" Jason said, grinning slyly.

"Together?" When he nodded, we both turned our cards over at the same time. Eyes wide, I glared down at his cards and both Jason and Will bellowed. "You have got to be kidding me. How the hell is that possible?"

Jason stood triumphantly as the dealer split the pot. We both had a six and a queen, which left us even. "At least you didn't lose." Taking my hand, he helped me up and smacked my ass. "You can earn some of that money back tonight." I gritted my teeth and smiled. Putting his arm around my waist, he handed me my chips and winked.

"All right, you two, it's time to play," Will called, nodding toward his table. His wife wasn't in sight, which sucked monkey balls because I wanted to talk to her again. I planned to grill her about Madame Chatfield to see if she'd admit they were sisters. For all I knew, she could be embarrassed by her sister's profession.

"Surely, you don't expect me to play," I commented.

Will looked back at me and winked. "Why not? You seem to know what you're doing. It'll be refreshing to play against a woman."

His friends stood when we arrived, along with Will's two bodyguards. Will placed a hand on Jason's shoulder and went down the line. "You already met my security, Butch and Tom. This right here," he said, pointing to the blond-haired, green-eyed pretty boy, "is Chazz Davies. He's head of the music department at Randall Industries. He finds the talent."

Jason and I shook his hand, but his gaze lingered a little too long on my body for my liking. I felt like a piece of meat being waggled in front of a pit bull.

"And this handsome man," Will continued, pointing to the serious man with dark hair and brown eyes, "is Mark Chamberlain. He does all of my team scouting. I think I'm up to ten teams already."

"Eleven now," Mark said, smirking.

"Impressive," I added.

Will smiled at me. "I'm glad you think so. Guys, Jason Avery and Aylee McFadden are going to join us tonight. Surely, there are no objections?"

Chazz held out a chair for me and Jason nudged me toward it, even though I could feel his hand tense on my lower back. I nodded at Chazz with a small smile. "Thank you."

He took the seat beside mine. "My pleasure. We don't get many women who play."

Will sat down across the table and snorted. "I'm pretty sure she knows what she's doing."

Jason's lip tilted up in a smirk. "That she does." Then he turned to Will. "We going to play with seven?"

Will nodded. "Drake couldn't make it tonight, but he'll be at the party tomorrow. Would you like to join us? I'm sure my wife would love to see the lovely Aylee again. All she could talk about was how gorgeous and sweet she was," he explained, smiling at me.

Jason put his hand on my thigh and squeezed. "Then we'd love to come. I'm sure Aylee can deal with me for one more night?"

I batted my eyes. "I think I can handle it."

Will's eyes brightened. "Great, then it's settled. Make sure you don't spend all your money tonight. You'll need it tomorrow."

CHAPTER 12

AYLEE

By the end of the night, Jason was on edge. The tension was so thick I could cut it with a knife. Honestly, I liked knowing he was protective of me. He wanted to beat the fuck out of Chazz Davies and a part of me wanted to see it. I could still feel the way he pressed against me earlier. My body wanted more, but I had to convince my mind.

"Jason, you okay?" I asked.

He opened the door to our suite and held it for me, before storming inside. He threw his jacket on the couch and huffed. "I'm fine, just a little pissed off." I caught his gaze in the window as he looked out at the city lights. "I know you're not mine and I know you're a strong woman, but when the others looked at you tonight, I wanted to tell them to back the fuck up. I want to protect you from them."

The air left my lungs and I froze. His words touched me in places I never thought I'd have feeling in again. "I could tell," I whispered. My heart raced in my chest, especially when I got the courage to touch his shoulder, to make that contact. I wanted to hear more. "Is that the only reason why you've been in a mood? Are you mad because you lost a round?"

He scoffed. "No, that's not a big deal. I can't always win."

"Then what is it? We're finally in the game we've been waiting on. Granted, we haven't met Drake yet, but this is a huge step for the case. The party tomorrow will be the perfect chance to get a feel for what they're really like."

Sighing, he turned to face me. "That's what I'm afraid of. I didn't like the way Davies looked at you. Just do me a favor and stay away from him tomorrow."

"*That's* what you're mad about? Really?"

Jaw clenched, he stood there, eyes blazing. "It was a stupid idea having you pretend to be a whore. Now those fuckers won't respect you."

"I don't think they'd respect me either way. They're douchebags. I could tell before they even opened their mouths. You knew this was going to happen."

"Yeah, but I didn't think . . ." he stopped, averting his gaze.

"Didn't think what?"

He stared up at me and all I could do was stare back. A woman could get lost in his eyes; they were so green. "I didn't think I'd feel this protective of you."

"Why do you? You don't even know me."

He brushed the hair off my face and stepped closer. "No, but I'm beginning to. And the thought of someone touching you or hurting you drives me goddamned insane. I wanted to break Davies' hand tonight."

I smiled and then bit my lip. "I wanted to break his hands too. I don't like being touched by strangers."

"Then I guess you don't like this," he said, slowly sliding his finger down my cheek.

My eyes closed briefly, but then I backed away, reluctantly withdrawing from his touch. "You're not a stranger, Jason."

"Then why won't you let me touch you?"

"We shouldn't be doing this. It'll only make things harder."

"I like things hard." Quite literally, his dick twitched against my leg.

"I can see that," I murmured.

"What do you say? We're here, we're together for however long . . ."

"I don't just sleep with men when I feel the urge,

Jason. I'm not the whore I'm pretending to be." I tried to pull away, but he grabbed me around the waist.

"I wasn't insinuating that you were. All I'm saying is that I want you and I don't know how long I can fight it."

My breath caught as he lowered his mouth to mine. Before we could connect, I splayed my hands across his back and he froze. "Jason, what happened?" I tried to lift his shirt, but he grabbed my hand, pulling it away.

"It's nothing, just the aftermath of an accident I was in a few years ago."

"Aftermath? Had to have been something bad to do that kind of damage."

He sighed, the pain clear in his eyes. I wanted to hear his story and he was just about to open up when my phone rang. I stood there, waiting, but he nodded toward my purse. "Don't you need to answer that?"

I looked over at my purse and huffed. "Probably, but I want to hear what you have to say."

"I'm pretty sure you don't." Knowing he wasn't going to say anything until my phone stopped, I stalked off and fetched it out of my purse. "Who is it?" he asked curiously.

I cleared my throat. "It's Adrian."

"As in your ex-boyfriend?" I nodded and his jaw clenched. "Don't let me get in the way then. I'll see you in the morning."

"Jason, it's not like that."

"No, it's okay. You said it yourself, if we let things go further it'll only make things harder." He stormed off to his bedroom and shut the door.

I had no clue what the hell I was going to do.

CHAPTER 13

AYLEE

The hotel door slammed shut and I regretted ever answering the phone. Jason had been on edge all night and the last thing he needed to do was go out and get into trouble. I feared his trouble would involve stuffing his cock deep inside another female. The thought made me sick, which surprised me. I guess I had some things to reassess.

"Adrian," I answered, hoping he couldn't hear the distress in my tone.

"Aylee, it's good to hear your voice. I've missed you."

"I've missed you too. How's it going up in Maine?"

"Good. I visit your uncle regularly. He misses you. I

told him I was going to call you and give you the good news."

"Oh yeah? What's going on?"

"I'm taking a job in New York. One of the hospitals down there needs a thoracic surgeon. The money is good and I'll be making way more than I am now."

"That's great. I'm so happy for you. I'm sad that I won't see you when I get home, but I know you'll love being in a bigger city." It was going to be lonely back home without him but he deserved the chance to grow.

"Which is why I'm calling. I know you don't want to hear this again since our argument before you left, but please just listen. With the money I'll be making, I can support you without you having to put your life in danger. I can be what you need me to be. If you want me to be adventurous, I'll climb mountains and go skydiving. I miss you, Aylee. Please think about it; think about coming to New York with me."

Sighing, I laid down on my bed, my chest aching. "I don't know what to say. I would never ask you to change, Adrian. You're smart, funny, and one of my closest friends. I do what I do because I love helping people, just like you."

"Will you at least consider my offer? I'm moving tomorrow. I'm leaving my address and a small present for you at your uncle's. If you don't come to New York, at least I know there'll be something here to take care of you."

A tear fell down my cheek onto the pillow. "You're too good to me," I cried.

"It's because I love you, I always have. No matter what you decide, I'll always be there for you."

"Thanks. I love you too. New York is a big city compared to Augusta, be safe on your move."

He laughed. "That's for damn sure. Be careful out there."

"I will." We hung up the phone and I sat there, debating on if I should go after Jason.

Instead, I changed into my pajamas and sat in the dark, drifting in and out of a restless sleep. Whether I dreamt it or not, I don't know, but there was a time in the dead of night where a set of arms wrapped around my stomach and held me close. Jason's scent engulfed me and I held onto him, breathing him in. I fell asleep fast and then woke up to the morning sun, alone. It had all been a dream, but I swore I could still smell him.

With my back turned, I could hear Jason coming up behind me. "Where did you go last night?" I asked, slicing my apple with a little too much force. We had an hour before it was time to leave for the big party and I had yet to see him all day.

"I needed to blow off some steam."

"I see. You must have been pretty angry for it to take all night."

"Trust me, I needed it."

Stabbing the knife into one of the apples, I turned and glared at him, his eyes widened. "I bet. Just make sure next time you let me know where you're going in case I need you. Not that I would want to encroach on your fuckfest, but we do have a job to do here."

"Fuckfest? What the hell do you think I did last night?" he asked, returning my glare.

"Oh, I don't know, probably screwed the first sea donkey who was willing to ride your cock."

"I've been out here for months, sacrificing my own pleasures for the sake of the job. I need the release. And what does it matter anyway? You let me go for your ex."

"It wasn't like that," I exclaimed.

"Oh yeah? And what was it like? I bet he told you he missed you and that you two should get back together." My face paled and his eyes narrowed. "Exactly."

"So what? What if he did say those things? It doesn't mean I told him I wanted him back."

He stepped closer. "And just because I went out last night doesn't mean I fucked the first girl who came my way."

"The second then," I countered.

His jaw clenched, but then he smiled. "I guess you'll

never know." Winking, he backed up with a smirk on his face. It made me want to smack the shit out of him. "I need to get ready for the evening. I have a date with a whore."

Grabbing a slice of my apple, I threw it at his head. "Ah, you're so goddamned infuriating. I think I'm beginning to hate you." It was a lie, but it felt good to say. If anything, it made me want him more. Shoving the remaining apple slices in my mouth, I trudged to my bedroom and slammed the door.

The dress I had picked out was silky and black and fell to the floor. I was tired of showing my legs, but this time it'd be the swell of my breasts and all of my back that would be on display. I hoped Jason choked when he saw me.

When the time came for us to leave, I emerged from my room with my head held high. Jason's mouth dropped open as I walked by him. Glancing over my shoulder, I caught him staring at my backside.

"Holy fuck. Make sure you stay by my side tonight."

"I can't promise that. As you said earlier, I'm a whore, so I guess I need to act like one."

He ran his hands over his face and groaned. "Only with me. Why do you have to make things so difficult?"

"The only person doing that is you. Can we go now?"

He motioned toward the door. "After you,

firecracker."

Huffing, I grabbed my purse and marched out the door. Jason caught up to me and grabbed my elbow. I tried to jerk away, but he held tight. "I thought we were getting along there for a while."

I snorted. "Yeah, well, you let your dick get in the way."

"I like all of this jealousy, it makes your cheeks red." He pinched my cheek and I smacked his hand away.

"Oh my God, you're seriously going to drive me bat shit crazy. And don't get me started on jealousy. Who was the one who stomped away when I got a phone call? To be one of the best agents in the country, you seriously need to learn more about women." I slammed my hand on the elevator button.

When it opened, Jason pushed me inside, guiding me until my back hit the wall. Gasping, I sucked in a breath, only for it to be cut off by Jason's lips. His body pressed into mine, holding me firm as he kissed me hard. My mind told me not to give in, but my body wanted him to take me. His lips tasted like liquor and mint. I would've given anything to get drunk from his kisses, but the elevator door dinged and opened.

Jason stepped back and rubbed the lipstick off his mouth, smirking. "You're right, I was jealous and I still am. I want you, but you're afraid to let me. The longer I'm around you, the harder it is to resist you. What makes it worse is, I *know* you want this just as bad as I do." He looked down at my chest. I followed his gaze and saw my hard nipples showing through the silky dress.

People started getting into the elevator, but we needed to get out. I brought my arms up to cover my chest. "Don't we need to go?" I whispered.

He stared down at my mouth and shook his head like he was clearing his thoughts. "Come on." The tension between us was so high, I could feel it tingling my skin. Jason had my hand in his strong grasp and led me to a parked limousine where the driver waited, wearing a black tux with his dark hair slicked back underneath a cap.

"Mr. Avery," he greeted with a nod.

"Good evening, James. You have the address, correct?"

He nodded and opened the back door. "We're all set to go."

Jason ushered me in and I scooted all the way to the edge, turning my body away from him as he got in. I was embarrassed with the way I gave into him so easily, but also unsure of what to do. With Adrian, everything was simple and slow; with Jason, it was all heat and moving very fast. I didn't know if I could keep up.

"Are you mad at me for kissing you?"

Not looking at him, I shook my head. "Shocked

really. I guess I wasn't expecting it."

"That's what makes it exciting."

I turned to him, my gaze serious. "That's what scares me. I've never felt that excitement before." Against my better judgment, I glanced down at his lips and the way he pulled the bottom one between his teeth. "And now I don't know what to do."

"I tell you what. Let's promise that once we get done with tonight, we'll go back to the hotel and talk. Nothing but honesty." The devilish gleam in his eye gave me pause.

"That doesn't sound so bad, but why do you look like that? You're up to something."

He shrugged. "You'll see, but I can guarantee you'll have fun."

Pulling up to Randall's estate, I wasn't surprised to see that his home was gargantuan, with a million cars in the lawn and driveway.

"I'm going to drop you two off at the front and hang tight until you're ready to leave. When you text me, I'll drive up to get you."

Jason handed the driver a wad of bills and patted him on the shoulder. "Thanks, James. I don't plan on staying here that long."

"No worries. I have plenty of things to keep me busy."

Opening the car door, Jason helped me out and I

straightened my dress. "Let's go meet Drake Blackwell, and see how much of a douche he is. If I had to take my pick on first impressions alone, I'd say Davies is the fucker we're looking for."

I couldn't argue with him there. "True, but Mark didn't really have much to say. You never know with those quiet types. It's hard to gauge their true nature."

Jason nodded. "I'll try to talk to him tonight, but I want to get a feel for Blackwell. Other than Randall, he's a powerhouse. Most of the time, these rich bastards think they're untouchable and they can get away with anything."

"True," I agreed. We got to the door and my heart raced. There was an ogre-sized man, dressed all in black, standing there with a list. He was even bigger than Butch and Tom with spiked black hair and dark skin.

"Name," he barked.

Jason stepped forward, squeezing my hand. "Jason Avery and Aylee McFadden."

Flipping through the list, he marked off what I supposed was our names and opened the door. "Enjoy your evening."

"Thank you," I offered as we walked by. When we got inside, my mouth flew open. The entry was huge and opened up to a large great room with hundreds of people milling about in their fancy clothes and jewelry.

I didn't come from money, but I knew how to play the part.

Jason leaned in close to my ear, his breath tickling my neck. "Stay close to me."

"I'll try, but if we get separated I'll be okay. Trust me."

Straight ahead, I spotted Chazz and a couple other men drinking at the bar. He lifted his drink at us and smiled; Jason growled low in his chest. "It's not you I don't trust."

"Aylee," a voice called out to my side. I looked over to find Diane Randall waltzing forward, dressed in a silvery flowing gown, her arms outstretched. "I'm so glad you made it. William told me you were coming." She grabbed my hands and kissed both my cheeks. "You look beautiful tonight." Diane seemed genuine in her actions, but it was hard to tell. I knew I needed to stay on my guard.

"Good evening, Mrs. Randall," Jason greeted.

She let go of my hands, but gently kept a hand wrapped around my arm. "Same to you, Mr. Avery. Do you mind if I steal Aylee away for a while? As I'm sure you can guess, I'd rather claw my eyes out than talk to some of the women here, but unfortunately, I have to play nice. It'd be good to have a woman around I know I can get along with."

Jason's jaw muscles ticked, but I glared a warning at

him. "Of course," he replied, keeping his gaze on mine. "I'll just take a look around."

Diane pointed down the large hallway. "If you go down that way, William will be in there with some of his friends. They're drinking brandy and getting ready for the game tonight. I'm pretty sure they'll invite you to play."

"If he does, can I watch?" I asked excitedly.

"Of course, my dear. I always watch the games. But I have to warn you, it's not the same as you'd see in the casinos. They play a little different."

Jason snorted. "I'm sure it's nothing I can't handle." He leaned down and kissed my cheek. "Have fun and I'll see you later." I nodded in reply and watched him as he took off through the crowd.

"Are you falling for him?" she asked, her voice amused.

I turned abruptly and chuckled halfheartedly. "I sure as hell hope not."

She smiled wide. "Well, if you aren't, I can definitely tell he's harboring feelings for you. He must be a good lover. Most girls in your situation can't wait to be away from their clients."

I shrugged. "I guess I just got lucky."

"Not many girls can say that. Hold onto him as long as you can. The majority of women in your business do this in hopes of snagging a rich man. Some achieve it, but a lot don't. Hopefully, Mr. Avery will offer you a lot more than just his money."

"How do you know so much about what I do? Were you one before you met Mr. Randall?"

She put a hand to her mouth to hold in her laugh. "Oh, darling, no. Believe me, I've been accused of being one since I have ties to that industry, but I've never dabbled."

"Ties?"

Pulling me over to a secluded corner, she grabbed two glasses of champagne off the waiter's tray on the way there. "My sister is Ronnie Chatfield," she confessed, her voice low. "It's not something we speak about much, especially now that some of her girls have gone missing and turned up dead. That's why I asked you if you were one of her girls the other day when we met. Anyway, do you see those women over there?" She pointed to a group of three women, all laughing with their fake smiles.

I nodded. "What about them?"

"They don't like it when my sister's girls come to the parties. I don't want them knowing you're a part of that crowd. Heaven knows you don't look or act like one, so I figured it'd be easy for you to play the part. Can you do that for me?"

"You mean pretend that I'm not a prostitute?" She bit her lip and nodded. "I'm sure I can handle that. But you don't take me as the type to care what people think."

She snorted and held onto my elbow as we strolled toward the women. "I don't, but unfortunately, their husbands work for William. I couldn't get rid of them if I tried."

As we approached, all three women eyed me up and down. Two of them were around my age with sleek hair and tight bodies, but the third woman was most likely in her early forties with fake tits and a body that screamed plastic surgery.

"Ladies," Diane announced, "this is Aylee McFadden. She's one of my guests." I shook their hands and said hello.

The third woman with chocolate brown hair took a sip of her wine and grinned. "It's nice to meet you Aylee. I'm Georgia . . . Georgia Blackwell."

A small smile splayed across my face. "It's nice to meet you too." And now all I needed to do was meet her husband.

CHAPTER 14

JASON

"Ah, you found us," Will announced, getting out of his chair. "Geoffrey, pour the boy a brandy, please."

I assumed Geoffrey was the man behind the bar because he pulled out a tumbler and filled it full of the amber liquid. He carried it over to me on a tray. "For you, sir."

Grinning, I took the glass. "Thank you." I finally got a good look at the men in the room and spotted Drake Blackwell immediately. All of my suspects were in the room together. What were the odds?

Will put his arm around my shoulder. "Gentlemen, this is Jason Avery, a kickass poker player I had the privilege of meeting. Not to mention, he spends a shit ton in my casino. I thought maybe he could join our game tonight."

"Did you bring money?" Drake asked.

I chuckled. "Don't worry, I came prepared."

His brows lifted and he stood, extending his hand. "I think I like this young man. I'm Drake Blackwell."

Taking his hand, I shook firmly. "Nice to meet you."

"And this," he said, gesturing to the man he'd been sitting with, "is my son, Blaine." He was the youngest out of everyone in the room, but most likely close to my age with light brown hair and hazel eyes like his father.

Blaine stood and shook my hand, grinning wide. "Nice to see someone who isn't ancient. You staying for the game tonight?"

"Don't know. Am I invited?"

"Only if you brought Strawberry Shortcake with you," Chazz said, glaring mischievously at me over the rim of his glass.

Blaine chuckled. "Strawberry Shortcake . . . am I missing something?"

Will sat down and smiled. "His date. She's quite a catch I might add. Definitely different from the women you see around here."

"And good at poker," Mark added. It was the first thing he'd said since being in the room.

"Are you into sharing?" Drake asked, a curious glint

in his eyes. All heads turned my way. Even Mark waited for my answer.

Tossing back the amber liquid, I felt the burn go all the way down. None of those fuckers were going to so much as touch her. "Not tonight, gentlemen. She's all mine."

As if on cue, she sauntered into the room beside Diane.

"Hot damn, is that her?" Drake asked, running his gaze down her body.

Chazz cut in. "That's her all right. Her name's Aylee McFadden."

Clenching my fists, I was about to slam Davies' face into the table, when Will cleared his throat. "And I suggest you keep your tongues in your mouths before Avery rips them out. She's taken for the night. Not to mention, my wife's in here, so show some respect."

Drake and Chazz both glanced at me with narrowed eyes and sat back in their chairs. Mark was the one who spoke next. "You said for tonight, but you didn't mention tomorrow."

"You're right, I didn't," I replied tightly.

Will huffed. "You're all drooling over this poor girl like rabid dogs. You know the rules, no gambling women unless they agree to it. If Avery wants to keep the girl to himself, that's his deal. Stop pressing the issue."

Aylee could sense the tension and glanced at me out of the corner of her eye. I wanted to pick her up over my shoulder and carry her out of the room so no one could think about her. I knew what was on their minds; it wasn't hard to guess.

"Miss McFadden," Drake called.

Gritting my teeth, I watched her gracefully walk over, her head held high, confident. Everything about her was intriguing. Instead of walking over to Drake, she walked over to me and sat down on the edge of my chair. "I must admit, sir, you have me at a disadvantage. You know my name but I don't know yours," she said.

He stood and extended his hand. "Drake Blackwell." Aylee took his hand and instead of shaking it, he lifted it to his lips. *Arrogant bastard.* "I wanted to see if you and Mr. Avery would like to join us at my house this weekend. That's where the true fun begins."

"I see, and what kind of fun are you talking?"

He smirked. "Let's just say you have to be willing to gamble with just about anything. You interested?"

Aylee turned to look at me, her gaze searching mine, but she knew it was what we had to do. Plastering on a fake smile, she focused back on Drake. "Sounds intriguing. I'll be there."

"Mr. Avery?" Drake asked, lifting his brows.

"Wouldn't miss it."

Will cleared his throat and stood. "All right, time to

play. Let's go, gentlemen . . . and ladies. Be prepared to empty your wallets tonight. I'm feeling lucky."

I wished I was; I felt the opposite. I was leading Aylee into a den of wolves, and I didn't like it at all. I had never failed on a mission and I wasn't going to let this one be my first. I had to protect her, no matter the cost.

CHAPTER 15

AYLEE

"Aylee, you know you don't have to go to Drake's," Diane whispered, concern in her voice.

I snapped back and gave her my attention. "Are you afraid something's going to happen?"

She sighed. "You seem like a smart, young woman and I know you can do more with your life than what you're doing. Why don't you come work for me? I'll pay you well and you won't have to worry about getting your money this way."

"What exactly do you do?"

"I design clothes."

I laughed. "That's the last thing you'd want my help

on."

"You wouldn't be designing clothes, silly girl. I'd hire you to be my assistant. I've always wanted one and since you and I get along so well, I think it could work. What do you say?"

Turning my body toward her, I spoke low. "You never answered my question. Are you worried something's going to happen to me?"

Her jaw clenched. "All I know is, girls are getting hurt and I don't want you going down that same path."

"Did you know some of them?"

"Not personally. I'd never talked to them like I do with you. They were focused on earning their money, not caring who or what they had to do to get it."

It was in that moment when I really got a good look at her. "Do you have kids, Diane?"

She sat back, her brows furrowed. "Why do you ask?"

"You're so much like my mother, or the way my mother was. She died when I was young. I never realized how much I missed talking to her until now."

Her eyes misted. "I'm sorry to hear about your mother. And no, we don't have kids. William and I weren't able to have any. With our work schedules, it probably worked out for the best. About next weekend though, what are you going to do?"

The game came to a close and the men stood.

Squeezing her hand, I looked into her eyes and said, "Don't worry about me. I know how to take care of myself."

Jason walked over and I caught a glimpse at the large bills he just stashed in his pocket. "You ready to go?" I nodded and took his arm. "Diane, it was a pleasure seeing you again," he said.

"Likewise." Then Diane focused on me. "I'd like you to consider my offer. How about next Monday we go shopping and I can give you a taste of what it is I do?"

"I'd like that."

She breathed a sigh of relief. "Good. I can pick you up at the hotel late morning. I'll give you a call Sunday to confirm."

More like confirm I was still alive. She knew something and I was going to make sure I figured out what it was. "I'll see you then."

She nodded at Jason and then glanced at me one more time before she took off toward Will.

"We have a lot to talk about," he murmured in my ear.

"You have no idea."

"Thank God, we're back," I stated, kicking my high heels off.

"No shit. Tonight was hard as hell. Having to listen to those cocksuckers talk about you made me so goddamned pissed I couldn't see straight. And we'll be right back into the thick of things this weekend."

"Isn't that what we've planned since the beginning?"

Sighing, he ran his hands over his face. "Yeah, but I've grown to care about you and it fucking blows. We need to talk about what we're going to do . . . what *you're* going to do."

"That's great and all, but I need to get out of this dress before I do anything else."

His eyes grew dark and heated as I walked toward the room, giving him my backside. I loved that I could get a reaction out of him. But what did it really matter? Any girl would turn his head.

Once in my room, I quickly changed into a pair of shorts and a T-shirt, making sure to put on my sexy bra since I couldn't wear it with my dress. When I got out of the room, Jason was in the living room with a deck of cards laid out in front of him on the coffee table. His button down shirt was halfway undone, showing the tattoos on his chest, tie hanging loosely around his neck. Diane was right when she called him sex on a stick. "What are you doing?"

"*We* are going to play cards, after you tell me about your conversation with Diane."

"Cards, huh?"

He glanced up, smirking. "It's a game I just invented. What I'm going to do is lay down a card in front of you and one in front of me. Whoever has the highest card gets to ask the other a question. It's called Draw of Truth."

"And you came up with this just now?"

"Yep, now have a seat so we can play. Unless you're scared."

Rolling my eyes, I sat down across from him. "Please," I scoffed. He set the cards on the table and gave me his full, undivided attention. "I think Diane knows something. She basically warned me not to go to Drake's this weekend. She even said I could work for her if I needed money."

He rubbed his chin. "Interesting. Anything else?"

"She also confessed to her sister being Madame Chatfield."

"Holy shit."

"That's what I thought too. She obviously doesn't have anything to hide, but there's still something I'm missing. She's really worried about me."

"Maybe you shouldn't go. I can always say you're sick, or with another client. We're getting too far in and I don't know how I'm going to be able to protect you if you run off with one of those fuckers. They're going to gamble for you. You do know that, right?"

Sighing, I leaned over on my elbows. "I figured as

much. I'm prepared to handle that."

He growled low. "How? If I have to watch any of them put their fucking hands on you I'll rip them off."

My head snapped up. "Jason, what's wrong with you? What makes you think I'm going to let them touch me? Reading your file, I had no clue you had such a volatile temper." I glared at him, but he averted his gaze.

"I'm sorry. For years, I've worked on my own and haven't had to worry about anyone other than myself. You keep saying you're prepared, but you haven't included me on any plans."

It was true, I hadn't. I wasn't planning on telling him what I was going to do, but I had no choice. I trusted him enough to know he wouldn't disclose secret government projects to just anyone. Getting to my feet, I rushed to my bedroom.

"Where are you going?"

"I'm going to show you something, so you know I'm covered." In my suitcase, there was a secret compartment holding the case I needed. There were six vials inside, all filled with a special clear liquid. Holding the case, I took a deep breath and carried it straight to Jason, setting it down in front of him. "This is it."

He looked down at it, pursing his lips. Carefully opening the case, he picked up one of the vials. "What's in it?"

I sat down beside him and pulled another one out.

"You know I work for the FBI, but you never asked what I did for them other than undercover work. This," I said, holding up the vial, "is what I work with. Not only did I study Criminal Investigation, but I was a whiz in Chemistry. For the past year, I've been working with a chemist in one of our labs. In this liquid, there's a sedative, a hallucinogen, and a new substance we found in Brazil that's like a form of ecstasy; it also increases your sexual responses." Clearing my throat, I set both vials back.

"Isn't that what we don't want?" he countered angrily. "These men are already ready to fuck your brains out."

I put my hand on his leg and moved closer. "I know, but in this exact combination, it has the ability to incapacitate the victim enough to where you can basically say anything to them and they'll believe it's true. I can make them believe we had sex even though we didn't take our clothes off or touch."

"What if you can't get it into their system?"

"I will. I can't think otherwise. I'll carry it in a syringe so I can either squirt it into their drink or drive it through a vein. Either way, I have to get it done."

"I still don't like this. Something could go wrong."

"You have to trust me, Jason. Trust I can do this without fail. Can you do that, please?"

"And where am I supposed to be while you're off

pretending to fuck these asswipes?"

"Hopefully, close. When the men are passed out, I'm going to search their houses, or wherever the hell they take me, for clues. The women had to have been killed somewhere, right?"

"True, so I just need to follow you to the location."

I nodded. "That way, after I search you can get me the hell out of there. Think you can keep up with us?"

A smirk splayed across his face. "I've already got it covered."

"Do I even want to know?" I asked.

He shrugged. "Probably not. Now get your ass over on the other side of the table. It's time to play."

Smiling, I moved over. "Draw of Truth?"

"You're damn right," he insisted, shuffling the cards again. "You ready?"

I waved him on and he laid down an eight of hearts and then a ten of clubs in front of me; I smiled. "I get to ask the question, right?"

"Yep."

"And how do I know you'll tell me the truth?"

His serious gaze bore into mine. "You'll just have to trust me, like I'm going to trust you."

"Good deal. Here's my first question . . . have you ever killed anyone?"

"Yes," he answered tightly. "During an underground fighting match a fucker pulled a gun on me. I made a choice."

"Is that the only time? Oops, wait, you can't answer that. That's more than one question."

He shook his head. "No, it goes along with the same one. I did kill someone else not too long ago. I don't know if you heard about the families who were murdered in South Carolina."

"That was just recently. Were you the one who found the killer?"

"Yeah. I don't know what came over me, but I fucked him up. I didn't want him to get out alive." Averting his gaze, I could tell it was hard for him to talk about it.

It wasn't easy killing another human being, but some deserved to die. I might go to hell for thinking that way, but it was the truth. I nodded and he placed down two more cards—my win. "What is it you love most about North Carolina?" I asked, hoping to change the mood.

He smiled, but it was sad. "My friends. Oh, and the weather. It's not hot as shit like it is here and it's not cold as fuck like it is up in Maine. It's perfect."

"I can't argue with that. But, on the other hand, we don't get the humidity. Our summers are perfect."

He laid another set of cards down and this time he won. My palms started to sweat and my heart raced; especially when he stared at me, smirking. "All right, firecracker. It's my turn. Do you still have feelings for your ex?"

That wasn't the question I was anticipating. Looking straight into his eyes, I said the honest truth. "Not in that way. We have a long history together, and I care about him as a friend. Any romantic feelings I had for him are long gone."

I could tell he wanted to ask more, but had to wait. Unfortunately, he didn't have to wait long because he won the next round. "Would you have let me fuck you if we didn't get interrupted by your ex? And you have to be honest."

I lowered my gaze and shrugged. "Yeah, I guess I would have."

"That's not a straight answer," he pointed out, his voice serious.

I looked up at him and bit my lip. "Fine. Yes, I would have slept with you."

"Why?" he asked.

I waved my finger at him. "Can't ask that, it's not your turn. Deal again." He dealt again and I won. This time I needed to think of something deep . . . and then it came to me. "When you kissed me," I began, watching him tense, "you pulled away when I tried to touch you. I know something happened . . . what was it?"

Very slowly, he unbuttoned his shirt, one button at a time, his gaze never wavering from mine. The pain in his eyes was evident and with each button he opened, I wanted to take back my question.

"Stop," I begged, getting to my feet. His fingers froze right before he was about to take off his shirt, his chest rising and falling with his rapid breaths. "Please, just stop. I never should've asked that question. I didn't realize how hard it was going to be for you."

He stood and faced me. "I'm not afraid to show you my scars, firecracker. It's the reason behind them that pains me." He slid off his shirt and I was finally able to see the rest of his tattoos and the contours of his chest and abs. His skin was perfect and tanned, smooth. Muscles tensing, he looked into my eyes one last time before turning his body around. From the front he was flawless, but from behind there was considerable pain, the aftermath of a horrible tragedy.

I stepped forward and reached out a hand, expecting him to recoil from my touch, but instead, he leaned into me. I traced the scarred flesh beneath my fingertips; he had been burned, badly.

"I don't know if you knew this, but I didn't just have one sister, but two, both younger. One is an undercover detective and the other was a rising beauty queen, literally. She was on her way to becoming Miss USA. The day before she was supposed to leave for the pageant, her friends threw her a party. She and my sister were on their way home when she swerved off the road to avoid a deer. Her car flipped and rolled into a ravine. I wasn't far behind them in my car so when I saw the accident, I tried to help.

"The car caught on fire, but I knew Braylen was dead. Brooklyn, on the other hand, was still alive. It took me forever to get her out, and just as I did, the car burst into flames. I got most of the damage shielding Brooklyn, but she too was burned. For years after that, my parents blamed me for Braylen's death. They were angry with me for not getting her out."

"But you couldn't. You said it yourself, she was already dead. It makes sense you would choose Brooklyn."

He laughed, but it wasn't meant to be humorous. "Braylen was their favorite. They didn't want to accept she was gone."

"Are they still mad at you?"

Turning around, he smiled down at me. "You're cheating. That's another question."

"It's actually a part of the original one," I countered.

"Well then, no, they're not mad at me anymore. It took them a while, but they came around."

"I'm glad. I bet that wasn't easy."

He set two more cards down and shook his head. "It wasn't. But now it's my turn." This time, he dropped the deck of cards onto the table and brushed his thumb across my lips. "If I tried to kiss you now, would you let me?"

He tilted my chin up, bringing his lips close to mine.

I could feel his breath and see the raw heat in his eyes. All I had to do was give him the answer and seal my fate. "I would say yes, but I can't. Not until I get one final answer from you."

"Which is?"

"Last night, when you left and didn't come back until dawn, did you sleep with anyone?"

He stared at me and then dread settled into the pit of my stomach when he nodded. "I did," he answered.

Anger boiled in my veins, and I pushed him away as hard as I could. "You son of a bitch. Get the hell away from me."

"Aylee, let me finish. It wasn't like that." He wrapped his arms around my waist to hold me in place, but I elbowed him in the side.

"Let me go!"

He growled in pain and even more so when I elbowed him again and rushed toward the door. The thought of him being with another woman made me furious. I was even more disgusted that he wanted to have sex with me the day after. "Dammit, Aylee, stop!" he shouted.

My hand touched the knob and before I could turn it, he grabbed me around the shoulders and tackled me to the floor. I tried to fight him off, but he held my wrists above my head, his body pressing into mine. "Let me up or I swear to God I'm going to cut off your balls and make you eat them."

"Now that I have your attention, you can listen to what I have to fucking say." I turned my head, not giving him the satisfaction of seeing I was hurt. "Look at me, Aylee," he commanded.

"Fuck you."

Tightening his hold, he held my wrists with one hand and grabbed my chin, forcing me to look at him. "My God you have a temper. One way or another, you're going to listen to me. I did not fuck another girl. I *slept* with someone, but I didn't fuck her."

"You expect me to believe that?" I spat.

His mouth pulled back into a smile and he moved closer, lips almost touching mine. "You need to believe it, considering the fact I slept next to *you*. I'm actually insulted you don't remember."

Eyes wide, I gasped, my body relaxing beneath his. I thought I dreamt about him in my bed, but I was wrong. Or maybe I subconsciously knew all along.

"You remember don't you?"

Pursing my lips, I rolled my eyes. "Talk about being a creeper. Maybe it's you I should be afraid of."

He chuckled low and whispered across my lips, "You should definitely be afraid." Letting my wrists go, he brought his mouth down on mine.

My mind was telling me to stop him, but I could only focus on the taste of his lips and the way his hands felt on my body. The next thing I knew, my shirt was off and his mouth was on the mounds of my breasts.

"You have no idea how bad I've wanted you." Pulling my bra back, he flicked his tongue across my nipple, forcing a moan from between my lips. Spreading my legs with his knee, he pushed his arousal into me and rocked.

I wrapped my arms around his neck and for a split second he tensed when I touched his scarred skin, but relaxed when I bit down on his ear. Our bodies rubbed together and that delicious ache I'd longed to feel again surfaced. My breaths came out in rapid pants and I held onto him tight, but he stopped and looked down at me.

"Before we go any further, is this what you want? I don't want you waking up in the morning thinking this was all a mistake."

"It is what I want, but I don't want to be another notch on your belt. What if *you* wake up tomorrow ready to move on to the next thing?"

With heat-filled eyes, he reached behind my back and unhooked my bra, sliding it off my body. My skin broke out in chills as he lowered his lips to a nipple and sucked. "That's not going to happen, firecracker. You keep me on my toes. I'm not letting you go, not until you want me to."

I smiled and bit my lip. "I'll let you know."

Hoisting me in his arms, I giggled and kissed my

way up his neck as he carried me into his bedroom. Tossing me onto the bed, he basically ripped my shorts off before sliding out of his pants. I shivered at the sight of his cock and ached to feel him inside me. He chuckled at my distress and prolonged it by kissing his way up my thighs, watching me the entire time. When he spread me wider, I held my breath until the first touch of his warm tongue across my clit made me jump.

"You like that?" he asked, licking me again.

"Very much so," I moaned, moving my hips against his face. With his mouth on my sweet spot and a finger inside me, I was in heaven. I didn't realize how much I missed the passion of intimacy. I'd never really had it before.

As Jason crawled up my body, I trembled in anticipation. I was glad he couldn't hear the pounding in my chest. It almost felt like I was having sex for the first time. He buried his face in my neck and kissed his way up to my lips, opening me with his tongue. "Do I need to wear a condom?"

"I'm on the pill," I moaned, arching my back as he massaged my breast.

Leaning down, he bit my nipple and growled, pushing the tip of his cock into my opening. I sucked in a breath and waited for him to slam into me, and when he did, I screamed out his name. His body slapped into mine and I countered by thrusting my hips up into his.

Growling deep in his chest, he dug his fingers into my hips and bit down on my neck. "Holy, goddamn shit, you're going to make me come so fucking fast."

I didn't care because I was about to explode all around him. Wrapping my legs around his waist, I could feel my insides clench and my orgasm build. "Harder," I begged.

He sat up and pulled me with him. With his knees spread he held me tight against his body and pounded into me so hard the bed slammed into the wall. "Fuck," he shouted. Grabbing my ass, he held me tight, bouncing me hard on his cock.

I wrapped my arms around his neck and pushed my breasts in his face as I threw my head back. My clit was now rubbing against his skin, making my release come quick. It was so strong my eyes rolled into the back of my head and my toes curled. With my pussy and hips spasming uncontrollably, Jason sped up his thrusts.

Grunting loud, he jerked and twitched, his warmth spilling into me. Breathing hard, he pressed his forehead to mine and kissed me. "That felt so fucking good."

"That it did," I said, smiling lazily.

Eyes sparkling, he lifted his brows. "Want to do it again?"

CHAPTER 16

JASON

"I really don't like this idea," I growled, getting into my car. For the rest of the week, I tried to convince her to back out of this plan, that I could handle it on my own, but she fought me at every turn.

Huffing, Aylee rolled her eyes. "We've been through this. You have to let one of the other men win, Jason. I'm going to leave all of my playing to you." The thought of intentionally losing a game so she could be thrown into the hands of another enraged me. It wasn't in my blood to lose.

"I know," I grumbled, gripping the steering wheel. "Keep your phone on you at all times. If I sense any trouble, I'm coming in after you."

She laughed and grabbed my hand, locking her fingers through mine. I loved the sound of her laugh. "There's not going to be any trouble, I promise."

Unfortunately, there was nothing I could do to get her to stay at the hotel. She was determined to do this and I'd come to realize there was nothing that was going to stop her. Even if I physically tried to apprehend her, she'd find a way out. She was that smart and determined.

We got to Drake's house all too soon and already my blood was on fire. Now that Aylee was mine, I didn't want any other man touching her. Out of all the cases I'd worked, this one was the hardest. I looked over at her in her emerald green dress and the way her tits moved up and down as she breathed. "Are you sure you don't want my coat?"

"Trust me, I don't like wearing this shit, but you know I can't cover up."

We got out of the car and headed for the door, passing only a handful of cars in the driveway. Drake's house wasn't nearly as big as Will's, but it was down the street and in the same neighborhood. The door opened as soon as we got to it and there stood Drake, smiling wolfishly at Aylee.

"Welcome," he announced, pulling her inside. "Would you care for a drink?"

She chuckled. "Already trying to get me drunk?"

"Not at all, darling." Then he looked at me. "How

about you? Whiskey? Bourbon?"

"Whiskey."

"Coming right up." He sauntered off and motioned for us to follow him. The hallway opened up to a ballroom of sorts, where a man played the grand piano and there were gambling tables everywhere with dealers.

"He has his own little casino," Aylee whispered.

"And how much you want to bet he pays the dealers to rip everyone off?" I held out my arm and she took it.

"Then I guess you don't have to worry about trying to lose."

Drake poured up a whiskey and handed it to me. "Got you a double. You look like you need it."

"You think?"

He chuckled. "I figured you needed to get loosened up before the game. Are you playing tonight, beautiful?" he asked Aylee.

She shook her head. "I'm going to let Jason play on my behalf. I was afraid you all would clean me dry. Besides, I don't have millions of dollars to hand over."

Drake's eyes went wide. "Well, aren't you a feisty one. I like that." He patted me on the shoulder. "Just don't get sore if you lose tonight. Agreed?" He held out his hand and I shook it, wishing I could punch him right in the nose.

"Agreed." Unfortunately, there were no other women in the room, so all eyes were focused on Aylee as he led her to a chair and helped her sit.

"Avery, right here," Drake called, patting the seat beside his at the poker table. There were only four of us at the table even though there were other men in the room. Clearly, they weren't invited to join. Across from me sat Chazz with an eat shit grin on his face. To my right was Drake who drank his Bourbon like it was water, and then to my left was Mark, his expression unreadable.

The dealer took his place and shuffled the cards. "Gentlemen, are you ready? No chips will be allowed tonight. Strictly cash, or whatever it is you want to bet."

"Hell yeah," Chazz exclaimed, slamming his hand on the table.

I glanced quickly at Aylee who smiled and winked at me. At least I didn't have to worry about her being ready for this. If I'd detected any hint of fear, I wasn't going to let her go through with this. I would drag her kicking and screaming back home to Maine.

The dealer passed around our first two cards and mine were more than pathetic. I had a two and five of hearts. Drake threw in a hundred dollar bill and instead of folding like I knew I should, I put a hundred in as well. Chazz and Mark followed suit. The dealer then put down the three card flop and much to my surprise ended up having two heart cards in the mix. If the last deal turned out to be a heart, I would have a flush. It

L.P. DOVER   125

was no surprise when Drake upped his bet to one thousand dollars. Reluctantly, I did the same and so did the others.

Smiling, the dealer dealt out the last card. *Fuck me.* It wasn't a heart and I was left with nothing but a pair of fives. Drake checked and I followed suit so I wouldn't have to up my bid. The other two checked and the round was over; Chazz won the pot. "Good round, gentlemen."

Round after round we played, gambling nothing but high bills. I actually won a few hands. Aylee watched the game like a hawk, studying the players. I knew the time was going to come when the real gambling would begin. The men were feeling me out, waiting for the perfect time to strike. It'd been two hours and still no request for Aylee.

Unfortunately, by the way Chazz was drinking, it was only making him bolder. He took a sip of his liquor and glanced at Aylee over his shoulder. "Why aren't you playing tonight?" he asked, slurring the words.

Drake cleared his throat. "She decided to give her playing rights to Avery."

He frowned and finished his drink. "I see. What a shame. I was really hoping to see you in action tonight. Maybe there's still a way."

She perked up and smiled. "Oh yeah, how's that?"

Chazz stood and circled her like a hawk ready to

strike its prey. "Why don't you be the prize for the next game? Sure money's great and everything, but nothing can beat the feel of a woman's touch."

"Surely, you can have any woman you want. Why do you have to gamble for me?"

This time Mark spoke up. "Because you're beautiful and not like the women he's used to. Not to mention, you're taken, which makes it all the more alluring."

"Eh, she's not exactly taken, are you kitten?" Chazz said, sliding his finger down her arm. "Women like you always choose the highest bidder."

She glanced quickly at me before facing him, forcing a smile. "Not all the time, Mr. Davies. But in this case, I'll accept the challenge, on one condition."

"Name the terms," Drake called out.

Moving her arm away from Chazz, she stood and swayed her hips as she walked over to the table. "Whoever wins gives me the money in the pot. That'll be my payment for the night. Do you all agree?"

We all nodded. Instead of going back to her seat, she sat down at the table to watch. The dealer passed out our two cards and I ended up with a king of spades and an eight of diamonds. Drake tossed in a thousand dollars and I did the same. Mark, on the other hand, raised it to three thousand. We all had a choice to make, either put in three or fold. Nobody backed down. The flop was dealt out next which ended up being a seven of diamonds, nine of hearts, and a six of clubs. I was close to getting a straight.

Drake put in another two grand and when it came to my turn, all eyes were on me. Grinning from ear to ear, I pulled out five thousand more dollars and threw it in the pot. Aylee's eyes went wide and her lips flattened to a thin line. She wasn't happy, but I had a plan.

"Damn, son, you came to play," Drake noted, throwing in his five grand, followed by Mark and Chazz. The chance of getting a straight was slim, but my plan was working. I knew they would give it all for a night with her. The dealer laid down the last card and to my surprise it was a ten of diamonds; I had my straight. "All in," Drake exclaimed, tossing a wad of money into the pot.

"How much is that?" I asked.

He smiled wide. "Twenty grand. I'm sure your little morsel is worth that and much more."

That she was, but I had no choice. Releasing a heavy sigh, I looked over at her and pushed my cards away. Chazz almost choked on the contents in his glass. "Are you seriously folding?"

I nodded once and sat back, folding my arms over my chest. Mark folded as well and pushed his cards to the side. Chazz, on the other hand, was happy to toss his money in. They flipped their cards over and it was no mistaking who the winner was. Drake had a full house and Chazz had a three of a kind.

"What the fuck," Chazz growled.

Drake stood and pushed the money toward Aylee. "Here you go, beautiful. I hope this satisfies you."

Batting her eyelashes, she glanced up at him. "Not as much as you will. I'm sure of it."

He bit his lip and devoured her body with his eyes. Looking down at his watch, he grabbed his empty glass. "I do believe it's time to call it quits for the night, gentlemen. If you wouldn't mind seeing yourselves out, Miss McFadden and I are going to excuse ourselves."

Aylee stood and winked quickly before grabbing her purse and leaving the room with him. If anything happened to her, I was never going to forgive myself.

CHAPTER 17

AYLEE

"You have a beautiful home," I told Drake. The paintings on the hallway walls were absolutely breathtaking, no doubt the taste of his wife or an interior designer. It made me wonder where his wife was this evening.

"Thank you. The years have been good to me," he replied with pride. He was actually a good looking man with his coiffed brown hair and hazel eyes, dressed in his expensive suits. On the inside was where he was a disgusting rat bastard.

I turned my head, rolling my eyes. "I see that." At least my purse was ten pounds heavier—compensation for risking my life. "Where are you taking me?" I followed him up the steps to another hallway, where he opened one of the doors and ushered me inside.

"My bedroom, beautiful. You must keep Avery a happy man for him to keep you around for as long as he has."

"We work well together, Mr. Blackwell. I can't say I've had that chemistry with any other man." I walked into the room and as soon as he shut the door behind me, I reached into my purse and pulled out one of the tiny syringes. "I would love to have a glass of wine," I said sweetly.

Drake loosened his tie and tossed it onto the floor. "Any preference?"

"A Riesling would be great if you have it."

He winked. "Coming right up. Don't go anywhere." As soon as he left, I walked around the room. It was obviously the bedroom he shared with his wife. There were pictures of her and him everywhere, including their son who was the same age as me. Grabbing my phone, I sent Jason a quick text.

Me: I'm fine. About to slip him the meds.

Jason: Be careful. I'll be close.

I put my phone away and waited for about twenty minutes before Drake entered the room. He sure took his precious time. "You were in luck, I had one bottle left. Not many of my guests prefer the Riesling." He set the glasses down and opened the wine.

"What can I say? It's been my favorite for years. Has everyone left?"

"Yep, and now we're locked in tight for the evening."

"Do you have security guards like Mr. Randall?"

He snorted and poured us both a glass of wine. "No. Personally, I think the putz has them to garner attention. Nobody ever threatens his life."

I shrugged, accepting the glass he held out for me. "You never know." His bedroom was enormous with a huge king size bed and sitting room. I ventured to the other side where there were pictures displayed over the fireplace mantle. Why the hell would anyone in Vegas want a fireplace in their bedroom? It was an inferno compared to Maine's weather. I could lay out in the sun at fifty degrees and not break a chill.

Drake sidled up behind me and rubbed his hands down my arms. Instead of moving away like I wanted to, I pointed to the pictures.

"Where's your wife?"

He cleared his throat. "She left this morning to go on one of her shopping binges in California."

"And she doesn't mind you sleeping around? Or is this our little secret?"

"What she doesn't know won't hurt her. Besides, she's never here. Her and my son don't get along."

"Oh, I was assuming it was her son too."

"No, he's from my first marriage. I married Georgia

about three years ago."

"And you're already cheating on her. How many times have you been married?"

Turning me around, he regarded me curiously. "You sure do ask a lot of questions. Are you nervous?"

Amused, I snorted and took a sip of wine. "On the contrary, Mr. Blackwell. I'm just not the type of girl to spread my legs without making you work for it."

Licking his lips, his eyes turned dark. "Mmm, I like this game." He unbuttoned his shirt and let it fall to the floor. "What do you want me to do first?"

His full wine glass was across the room on his dresser along with my purse. With the syringe in the palm of my hand, I side-stepped him and strutted over to his glass, swaying my hips the whole way. As fast as I could, I squirted the liquid into his wine, hiding the syringe behind my purse. I swished it around and carried it over to him.

"What I want you to do first is start off with a toast." I handed him the wine, holding up my glass. "To a fun filled night we won't forget." Tapping my glass with his, he kept his eyes on me as he drank the full glass of wine. In the lab, it took five minutes for the sedative to work. Unfortunately, I had to get him on the bed before he passed out. He swayed on his feet and I quickly took his glass before he could shatter it on the floor. "I think someone had a little too much to drink tonight," I teased.

Lifting his hand, he ran his fingers through my hair. "I'm just ready to get the party started. Ever since that first night I saw you, I've been dying to get your legs wrapped around me."

I had four minutes left. I could see the numbers counting down in my mind. "Now's your chance, big boy. Why don't you get on the bed and let me do the rest of the work?" He fell down on the bed and chuckled as I unbuttoned his pants and pulled them off. His cock was rigid and pulsating just as I expected. All it would take is a simple touch and I'd have him ejaculating all over the place. If the world knew what I had concocted, it'd be a dangerous drug. I crawled up on the bed and laid beside him, running my fingers up and down his chest. His eyes started to roll back in his head and I smiled; it was almost time.

"You feel so good," he mumbled, slurring the words.

Once his eyes fully closed, it was time for action. Taking his own hand, I placed it over his cock and he unknowingly gripped onto it, jacking himself off. Thank God for hallucinogens. "That's right, baby. Do you feel me riding your cock? Am I tight enough for you?"

Drake mumbled something unintelligent and grunted when he ejaculated all over his stomach and chest. What would've been funny is if it shot up on his face. *Deserves the fucker right.* He was out for the count and there was nothing that was going to wake him up for at least five hours.

"When you wake up, you're going to remember this night as the best sex you've ever had. I made you come no less than three times and I won't walk right for a week." Covering him up, I slid off the bed and tiptoed to my purse, making sure to tuck the syringe safely inside before leaving.

By the time I straightened my dress and turned out the light, Drake had begun to snore. Slipping out of the room, I took off down the hall, pulling the small flashlight out of my purse. I knew very well a killer wouldn't just murder someone out in the open. They'd do it in a room with limited access.

However, everything about Drake didn't scream 'whore murderer' to me. To be such an aggressive businessmen, he was actually passive, even before being drugged. Sometimes the killer could be someone you least expected, but I couldn't see Drake being it at all. Pulling out my phone, I updated Jason.

Me: Blackwell is out. Searching his house.

Jason: How long?

Me: Out front in 15.

The house was quiet with no sound coming from anywhere as I descended the stairs. The lights were still on so I shut off my flashlight, hoping like hell there wasn't anyone around. I checked the rooms, one by one, and nothing peculiar jumped out at me; at least, until

I got to the kitchen. There was a door that had a set of wooden stairs, leading into the darkness.

Every time I watched scary movies, I would always scream at the people to stay away from the fucking basements. Unfortunately, I couldn't. At least there was a light switch on the wall that illuminated everything. The walls were made of stone and by the smell of earth and dirt I knew I was going underground. The floor below was made of stone so when I got to the bottom, I took off my heels to keep them from clanking.

There were no light switches for the darkened hallway but when I took a step, the light above shone bright. Lights were aligned down the hallway and as I walked the rest of the way, they lit up ahead and turned off behind me. At the end, the room opened up to reveal ceiling to floor shelves filled with champagne, wine, and beer. My uncle would be in heaven if he could see the exuberant amounts of expensive wines. There were bottles that cost over five grand a piece. With the amount of money I made I could buy him any wine he wanted for the bed and breakfast.

Taking one last glance around, I walked back down the hall. There was nothing that made me believe anyone had been tortured or killed down there. I grabbed my heels and carried them up the steps, lightly shutting the door when I got out. My time was up and I knew it because my phone was buzzing incessantly in my purse. Rushing to the door, I quietly snuck out and saw Jason on the other side of the gate, leaning against his car. Thankfully, there was a button on my side of the gate that opened it.

"Find anything?"

We both got in the car and sped away. "Nothing except over a million dollars in champagne and wine in his cellar. It was a dream come true."

"Is that the way to your heart?" he teased.

"Maybe my uncle's, but you don't swing that way. I'm sure if you ever met him he'd think you were the cutest thing." He smiled, but I could tell he was on edge. "And no, I really didn't find anything. I don't think Drake's our man. So now I have to find a way to get with Chazz and Mark."

He growled low. "And those two are the ones I'm worried about."

"What are we going to do now?"

Reaching for my hand, he clasped it tight. "Right now, we wait for the next game."

"What about the woman who's still missing? How are we going to find her?"

He glanced over at me, his eyes weary. "I honestly don't know."

A loud knock on the door woke us from our deep sleep. Jason grumbled under his breath and tightened his hold. "Whoever it is can go the fuck away. It's not even morning yet."

I rubbed my eyes and looked at the clock. "It's ten o'clock," I laughed. Then Jason's phone started to ring, and when he didn't pick up, mine started to howl. "I'm thinking I need to answer that." I evidently didn't get to it in time, as a text came through.

Ryan: Answer the fucking door!

"Holy shit balls, it's the chief," I grumbled. I didn't have any clothes in Jason's room so I jumped out of bed and grabbed a bathrobe. Jason threw on a pair of shorts and started for the door before I could join him. I tied the robe as fast as I could and rushed out, but Jason had already let Ryan in. His eyes went wide, glancing back and forth at us.

"Well . . . it seems like you two are getting along."

Cheeks burning, I ran a hand through my hair, hoping I didn't look like I stuck my finger in a light socket. "It took a while, but we worked everything out."

Jason crossed his arms over his chest. "What's with the visit? Did you find the missing woman?"

Ryan took a seat and sighed. "We did, but I also wanted to hear your progress. You two seem to be too busy lately to give me an update."

Jason and I sat down on the couch, facing him. The

last thing I wanted to hear was that the woman who went missing was found dead and mutilated. Instead, Jason answered him, "We've gotten close enough to Blackwell to check him out. Everything seems good with him. We have the other two left, but they shouldn't be a problem."

Ryan nodded. "Good."

I spoke up next. "What about the woman? You said you found her. What happened?"

Throwing his hands in the air, he shook his head, chuckling. "She went off and got fucking married."

Jason and I looked at each other and then back to him. "Married? So she's alive?" I asked.

"Yep. Apparently, she met this guy at a casino and they tied the knot. Her fiancé back home found out and is on his way out here now. Big mess."

I breathed a sigh of relief. "At least she's not dead."

He chuckled. "Not yet, but her newfound husband might be once the fiancé comes into town."

"But other than that, there's no other missing women."

"Right," he said, nodding. "Not until someone tries to take you."

CHAPTER 18

AYLEE

"Are you sure you want to spend the day with Diane? You could stay here with me and we can . . ." Jason came up behind me and pressed his arousal into my back, making me giggle.

"I told her I'd see her today. I'll be back this afternoon. Besides, maybe I can dig up more gossip. She's been a big help without her even knowing."

Tilting my head, he brushed my hair to the side and kissed my neck. "True. Just be careful. I might go downstairs and press my luck."

Finishing the last touches of my makeup, I smiled at him through the mirror; his emerald green eyes stared back, making me shiver. I wanted to spend the day in bed with him, but our duties took precedence.

"Is it bad I feel guilty about taking everyone's money the other night?"

He turned me to face him and I put my arms around his waist. "You shouldn't. You deserve way more than what you got. You risk your life every day at work, I wouldn't feel bad in the least. However, if you want to give me back what I put in that's fine. I'm sure we can have ourselves a little bit of fun with it."

"Oh yeah?" I said, lifting up on my toes. "It's a date." I looked down at my phone and realized I only had ten minutes before I needed to meet Diane in the lobby. "Yikes, gotta go." He kissed me quickly and I slid on my sandals before heading to the door. It felt great to wear normal clothes for a change.

I looked back and he smiled. "Have fun, firecracker. Text me if you run into any problems. I'll come save you."

"What if you don't know where I am?" I countered.

His grin grew wider and he winked. "I always know where you are."

"Okay, stalker. Don't make me have to get a restraining order." I winked back and grabbed my purse. "I'll be back soon."

"Do you have your gun?"

I patted my purse. "It's just like my Chapstick, I never leave home without it."

Once out the door, I hurried to the elevator and checked my phone; I wasn't late yet. When the doors opened, there Diane stood, dressed in a pair of khaki dress pants and a nice top. Even dressed like a normal person you could tell she was a woman of power. That was where I fooled people. Most wouldn't believe I was an FBI agent or that I'd killed before. To them I was just an innocent looking redhead who wouldn't harm a fly. Little did they know I'd squash any bug that came my way.

"Diane," I called, waving.

She turned my way, her smile brightening. "Look at you! I like your top. I designed one almost similar. When we go to my shop I'll let you pick one out. But I have to say, the green looks great with your hair."

"Thanks. So what are we doing today?" I followed her outside to a shiny, silver Mercedes waiting by the door.

She put on her sunglasses and walked around to her side. "Get in and you'll see."

When I got in the car, it still smelled new. "New car?" I asked.

She laughed. "Not really. I just never drive it. William got it for me after I had my hysterectomy. He thought it would make me feel better."

"And does it?"

"I don't know yet. That's what I'm going to figure

out. You hungry?"

"Starved." My stomach growled, proving my point.

"Great! There's this small café I like to eat at. It's nothing fancy, but on Mondays they make their broccoli and cheese quiche. It's to die for."

It only took about fifteen minutes to get there and when we walked in, the young hostess immediately sat us at a table in the back. "Do you and Mr. Randall always get special treatment everywhere you go?" I asked matter-of-factly.

She chuckled. "Only at the places we own, darling. I'm not one to like stomping on others just to get ahead. Sometimes we have to wait just like everyone else."

I glanced around the café, at the quaint doilies and the shimmering crystal glasses. It reminded me so much of the restaurant we had at the bed and breakfast. "You own this place?"

"I do."

"Wow," I uttered in amazement. "You and Will own a lot. How did you get started?"

"Basically, I had money and William had brains. Before his company even got started, I had the clothing line that's now extended to other cities and this restaurant. My family gave him some money to invest and he just kept earning it back. It amazes me how resourceful he is."

The hostess came back, smiling cheerfully. "Have

you had a chance to look over the menu?" she asked.

"I haven't, but I heard the broccoli and cheese quiche is to die for. I'll have that and a glass of iced tea, please."

Giggling, she took my menu. "I see Mrs. Randall's turning you over to the dark side. Once you've had our quiche you'll come back for more."

She strolled off and Diane smiled. "If you work for me, we can come here every Monday."

"I sense you're not going to give up easy, are you?"

Averting her gaze, her smile faded slightly. "I just think you owe it to yourself to explore other talents . . . safe ones."

"I'll think about it." It wasn't exactly a lie because my real job was dangerous, but I had lots of other options to choose from in my field. With the way I was making money in Vegas, I could live off of that for a few years and not worry about a thing.

Once our food came, all talk ceased until we finished our lunch and headed out the door. I could tell Diane felt like she overstepped a boundary. If only she knew I wasn't really a prostitute. "Do you still want to see my shop?" she asked.

"Of course. Let's go. It's fun hanging out with a woman. I'm so used to men."

"Do you . . . um, do you ever sleep with women?" The thought alone made me burst out in laughter. I laughed so hard a tear slid down my cheek. "I take that as a no?" she said meekly.

"Not just no, but hell no. I don't swing that way. Why do you ask?"

She shrugged. "Just curious. I know my sister's girls get contracted out to both men and women, sometimes both of them at the same time. They have to be willing to sleep with whoever is presented to them."

I shook my head. "Not me. I'm a one man kind of gal."

"All the more reason for you to work for me. You wouldn't have to worry about all of that. I'm sure Mr. Avery would love to keep you for himself."

At least for now he wanted me all to himself, but as soon as the case was over we'd go our separate ways. I really didn't want to think about that. "Jason and I live two separate lives. There's no way it could work."

"Will that bother you?"

We drove back down to the strip where a whole line of shops sat with hundreds of tourists walking around. I wanted to leave this place, but I couldn't imagine not ever seeing Jason again. "Yes," I answered truthfully, turning to look at her, "I'll miss him."

Smiling sadly, she parked her car and we got out. "Things always work out one way or another. It wasn't easy at first with William, but we managed to get through."

We started down the street and I looked up at the

buildings. "Which one's yours?" I asked. And as soon as I asked it, she pointed to a place up ahead. There was a store with her name on it in big bold letters. "Never mind, I see it now. I guess I should've looked harder." She snickered. "So what kind of clothes do you design?" I already knew since I had researched her thoroughly along with her husband.

"Anything and everything basically. I don't like to stick with just one style. I design from casual on up to elegant, winter and summer. Even if you don't care much about fashion, I'm sure we'll find you something you like."

As soon as she opened the door to her shop, the ladies all brightened and stood straighter. The place was two stories high, filled top to bottom with clothes. "Wow," was all I could say.

A tall, blonde with a huge smile stepped forward. "Good afternoon, Mrs. Randall."

"Thanks, Emily. This is Aylee McFadden," she said, turning to me. "Aylee, this is Emily. She's the manager of this branch. I'm sure if you decide to work with me, you two will be spending a lot of time together."

I held out my hand and Emily took it. "It's nice to meet you."

"Likewise. Whatever job she's offering, take it. She's really good to her employees. I've been here for fifteen years."

Diane put her arm around my shoulders. "See? I make a good boss. Now, let me show you around." We walked around her store and I had to admit, some of her clothes I'd consider wearing. She kept grabbing things left and right, folding them over her arm. Was she getting them for me? Surely not, but they did happen to be in my size. When she was done, she opened up one of the dressing rooms and pushed me inside. "Here you go," she said, handing me the bundle of clothes. "Try them on and whatever you like you can keep."

Eyes wide, I gaped at her incredulously. "You can't be serious. There's probably about eight hundred dollars worth of clothes here."

She smirked. "More like a thousand."

"Holy crap, that's insane. I can't take any of this."

"You can and you will. I'm your elder, so no arguing." Grinning from ear to ear, she winked and shut the door.

One way or another I was going to find a way to slip her the money. Instead of trying on the clothes, I pulled out my phone.

Me: I hate shopping!

Jason: Try on some clothes and take pics for me.

I took a picture of me flipping him off and sent it.

Jason: That's my girl. Lol! I'm in the Randall Enterprises lounge.

Me: WHAT? Why?

Jason: Drake wanted me to come by. I have a feeling it's about you. Pray that I don't kill the fucker.

"Shit balls."

Diane knocked on the door. "Aylee, you okay in there?"

Did I just say that out loud? "Yeah, I'm fine," I replied quickly.

"Okay, just asking. I thought I heard you say something. Anyway, I want to see that floral dress on you. I think it'll look amazing with your skin tone."

Throwing the phone in my purse, I quickly undressed. "Be right out, give me one sec." I slid the dress on and grunted, trying to get the fucking zipper pulled up.

Diane laughed. "Do you need help?"

Opening the door, I turned around. "I can't get it zipped."

She lifted the zipper and put a hand on my shoulder, speaking to my reflection in the mirror. "You look so beautiful. Times like these make me wish I had a daughter." Her eyes started to grow teary.

"It's an exquisite dress. You have an amazing collection." Just then, something out of the corner of my eye caught my attention.

"Aylee, are you all right?"

I forced a smile. "Yeah, of course. I'm just going to change."

She grabbed the clothes that were in the room, grinning mischievously. "I'll just get these packaged up for you." Before I could protest, she slammed the door and I could hear her giggling all the way to the register. There was no way in hell I could get out of there without Diane wanting to introduce me to her sister.

Me: Trouble. Madame Chatfield is here!

Jason: Shit!

Me: What if she recognizes me?

Jason: Play it cool. I'm sure you'll know what to do.

I finished getting dressed and took a deep breath. I didn't have a choice, I was going to have to leave the dressing room.

Diane was at the desk talking to Madame Chatfield with three big bags full of my clothes at her feet. There was no way in hell I could sneak out. "I'll take that for you," Emily offered, reaching for the dress.

"Thanks," I said, handing it to her. She sauntered off toward the desk and put it in one of the bags, drawing Diane's attention.

"There you are. I thought you got lost in there. I want you to meet someone. Veronica, this is Aylee. Aylee, this is my sister, Veronica." Ronnie must be her nickname.

Smiling wide, I strolled over and held out my hand. "It's nice to meet you."

She shook my hand, furrowing her brows. "Likewise,

my dear. I've heard a lot about you. I believe my sister has taken you under her wing."

"That she has and she's very persistent. I hope it was all good things you heard."

Letting my hand go, she searched my face, raking her gaze down my body. "Of course. Have we met before? There's something familiar about you."

"Not that I know of." The back of my neck started to sweat so I grabbed my hair and pushed it off to the side. Her eyes went wide and it didn't take long to figure out my mistake.

"It's you," she whispered, clutching her purse tight. "What the hell are you doing with my sister? She has nothing to do with this."

Diane stepped back, cautiously glancing at me while I tried to figure out how to get us out of there without a scene. "What's going on?" she asked.

Ronnie pointed to me. "She's an FBI agent. I recognize her from the scar. She forced her way into my car the other day and scared Harold half to death."

Gritting my teeth, I glared at her. "Keep your voice down. Right now isn't the place to discuss this. I'm one of the good guys, remember?" Then, blowing out a sigh, I turned to Diane, her gaze weary. "I need you to trust me. Can you do that?" She glanced quickly at Veronica and then gave a swift nod to me. "Good, let's get out of here and I'll tell you everything."

She grabbed the bags of clothes, but I stood in her way. "You know I can't accept those," I told her.

She stood firm, pursing her lips like a mother scolding a child. "And what did I tell you about respecting your elders? You're going to take these clothes even if I have to shove them up your ass. It's the least you can do for lying to me."

Storming toward the door, I let her go and hung back with Ronnie who laughed under her breath. "You've done pissed her off now, child. At least this time it's not me who did it."

"Gee, thanks." We walked outside and right out front was her limo, with Harold waiting by the back door, talking to Diane. Before getting to the car, I stepped in front of Ronnie, blocking her path. "I need a favor."

"Like what?"

"If I'm putting my identity on the line, I need something in return. I need to talk to your girls. There are a couple of men I'm investigating and I want to know who have spent time with them."

"Are you going to tell them you're with the FBI?"

"No, I'm going to pretend I'm just like them and interested in working for you. It's come down to the point where I have to find out more about these men. We can't lose another girl."

Sighing, she pushed me toward her car. "Let's go then."

We all got in and as soon as Harold shut the door, Ronnie lifted the privacy window. Across from me, Diane was on the edge of her seat, waiting for the window to seal us off. I counted down the seconds until she blasted off on me. *Three . . . two . . . one.*

"I can't believe this whole time you've looked right in my face and blatantly lied to me. Is your name really even Aylee?" she asked, her voice laced with hurt.

"Yes, my name's Aylee McFadden. I didn't want to lie to you, but it's my job. I know my betrayal hurts, but I had to find out as much as I could about the people I'm after. I have a feeling you already know something by the way you tried to keep me from whoring myself out to your friends."

Her eyes went wide. "Drake? You didn't . . ."

"Have sex with him?" I finished, watching her cringe. "Hell no. I searched his house and couldn't find anything. I'm not ruling him out just yet. Unfortunately, I have others to investigate as well."

Ronnie spoke up next. "And how do you think the police got the tip off about those men?"

I looked over at her. "Other than the eyewitness, I don't know. They didn't reveal the source." She nodded over at her sister. I gaped at Diane, completely in shock. "It was you?"

She sighed. "I see William's friends with Veronica's girls all the time. Sometimes they'd be passed around multiple times in the same night. When they started turning up dead, I kept getting this uneasy feeling in my gut. The guys didn't seem to care their playthings were being killed. They'd simply move onto others."

Ronnie patted my leg. "My girls know their profession is dangerous. I've lost a couple over the years, but never four within six months. When Diane and I started getting suspicious, that's when I temporarily shut down my business. I wasn't about to lose anymore girls, but it doesn't matter what I do, I keep losing them."

"That's why *I* called the police," Diane confided. "I didn't want William to know I was doing it, so I made sure to keep my name anonymous. He refuses to believe that any of them could be capable of murder."

"You don't think he has anything to hide do you?" I asked regretfully.

"No," she exclaimed, shaking her head, "not my William."

"But you haven't told him about your conversation with the police?" She shook her head. "Does that mean you'll keep today a secret from him too?"

"Yes. The more people who know about you, the more dangerous it's going to be. The thought of you doing this alone . . ." She paused and put a hand over her mouth, eyes wide. "Oh my God, you're *not* alone. Jason's with the FBI too?"

I shook my head. "He's an undercover cop I had the

privilege of meeting when I took on this case. As soon as it's all over, we'll go back to our regular lives."

"But you've fallen for him, haven't you?" Diane inquired.

Averting my gaze, I focused on the city view sweeping past the windows. I hadn't known Jason long, but my heart hurt knowing that one day soon I wouldn't be with him anymore. At least for the time being, I didn't feel alone. It was an amazing feeling. "It doesn't matter. I'm here to do a job. What happens in Vegas, stays in Vegas, right?"

CHAPTER 19

JASON

"Jason?"

I glanced over my shoulder at the younger version of Drake Blackwell. "Blaine, right?"

He held out his hand. "The one and only. I heard you were coming by today. Where's your lady friend?"

I shook his hand and laughed. "Doing what women love most."

"Ah, shopping. I know how that goes. If you want, you can follow me. I'll take you to my dad's office."

I followed him down the hall until we got to the end. He opened the door just as Drake finished a call and stood, extending his hand. I shook firmly, smiling when I felt his knuckles crack.

"Got a hard grip there don't you, son?"

"You know better than I do, you can't be a limp-wristed bitch in this business."

Tossing his head back, he bellowed, "You're completely right. See, I knew I liked you. I didn't take you away from the poker tables this morning, did I?"

"Nah, I figured I'd take a break. What can I do you for?"

"I thought I'd see if you wanted to catch lunch with me and some of the guys. You interested?"

"Sure. Where we going?"

Waggling his brows, he reached for car keys. "You'll see. Come on. You can ride with me and Blaine."

As we made our way to the door, Blaine excused himself. "Actually, I have a meeting with Tim Forrester on his new building project. I'm supposed to meet him in fifteen minutes."

"Good deal, that's what I like to hear." Blaine nodded and disappeared down the hallway. "Ready to go?" Drake asked.

"After you." I followed him to the elevator.

"Where's Aylee today?"

We got in and the door closed. "She's spending the day with Diane Randall."

"That Diane is a looker too, isn't she? I've always told Randall he was a lucky man."

"You're wife is beautiful as well," I told him. Well,

she would be if she wasn't as fake as a plastic doll.

He snorted. "You want her? I'll trade her for Aylee."

"Nah, that's okay. I'm happy with my choice."

We got off the elevator and walked out to the parking lot, straight to a black Maserati. "How long are you going to be in town?"

Opening the car door, I got in and he started up the car. "I don't know. Probably not much longer, why?"

"Just curious as to how long you'll be keeping Aylee to yourself. I have a list a mile long on the men who want a piece of her."

Clenching my fists, I focused on the fact that nothing happened between them. "Are you one of them?"

He chuckled. "How could I not be? She was the best fuck I've had in a long time. I don't see how you ever agreed to let her go."

"Trust me, I didn't want to, but she has a fiery temper to match that hair of hers. Besides, I'm not her owner. She's free to make her own choices."

"I'm having another party Saturday night. Do you think she'd be willing to be the prize again?"

"I don't know, I'll have to ask her." The thought pissed me off. I couldn't wait to get myself and Aylee the fuck out of Vegas for good. There was no way in hell I was coming back unless I *had* to. He pulled us into the parking lot of our destination and I tried my best to hide my impatience. We were at a fucking strip club that was also a steakhouse. "Lunch, huh?"

He winked. "What's a steak without a lap dance? Come on, it'll be fun." Unfortunately, fun didn't cover it. Chazz and Mark, along with three other men waited outside the door and smiled as we approached.

Chazz walked up to us. "Did Blackwell ask you about Saturday?" he asked, sounding hopeful.

"About the poker game or Aylee?" They were fucking obsessed with her. I guess I couldn't say much because I was enamored as well.

Drake put his arm around him and smiled. "She'll be there, my friend. Don't worry, you'll all get your turn."

Mark acknowledged me with a nod and walked inside while I followed behind them, seething. They weren't going to fucking touch her.

"Damn, Avery, you had all the ladies lining up for your cock today," Drake exclaimed as we left the club. Under normal circumstances, I would've been hard up having them dance on my lap, but I didn't give a shit about those women. "You should've let them take you to the VIP room."

"And why would I do that when I have my own piece of ass at the hotel, ready to pleasure me anytime I want? Those women don't compare. Besides, who honestly likes leaving a strip club with a hard on. Definitely not me."

He chuckled. "You have a point." It was three o'clock by the time we got back to Randall Enterprises. We got out of the car and I headed toward mine. "Saturday night you'll be at my house, right?" he called out.

I turned and waved. "Wouldn't miss it." As soon as I got in my car, I pulled out my phone. Alyee still hadn't texted an update.

Me: You okay?

Aylee: I'm fine. But you will not BELIEVE the shit I just found out. I'll be back soon.

After thirty minutes of waiting in the hotel room, I heard her slide the key card in the door. When she walked in, she had three huge bags full of clothes. "I thought you hated shopping," I taunted.

Groaning, she dropped her loot to the floor. "I do. But at least now I won't have to go shopping for the next decade."

"How much did that shit cost?"

Throwing her purse on the counter, she trudged over and wrapped her arms around my neck, smiling wide. "They were really expensive. I hope you don't mind, but I swiped your card this morning before I left."

I grabbed her ass and squeezed, making her yelp. "I know you wouldn't be stupid enough to do that."

Eyes wide, she kissed me quickly and let me go. "I

have so much to tell you."

I sat down and huffed. "So do I."

Instead of sitting on the couch, she sat down on the coffee table in front of me. "You go first."

"We got invited to Drake's party on Saturday night. Apparently, according to Drake, you were the best fuck he'd ever had. Now the others want their turn."

She grimaced. "It makes me feel dirty just hearing that. Are they playing for me again?" I nodded. "Okay, good. I'll join the game this time. Anything else happen?"

Smirking, I grabbed her hands. "I went to a strip club. Does that count as anything else?"

Her eyes narrowed. "Did you have fun?"

I shrugged. "Not really. You see, it's not as fun getting a lap dance when you're not going to bring the girl home and fuck her. I don't see the point in it anymore."

"So you *didn't* get any lap dances?"

Pulling her onto my lap, I bit her bottom lip. "That's exactly what I'm saying, firecracker. Why would I want those women when I am coming back here to you?"

Her lips drew back in a smile. "Smart man. While you were off at a strip club, I was actually at a whorehouse. I guess I can't get pissed, huh?"

"Whorehouse? Did you go to Chatfield's?"

She nodded. "Ronnie recognized me by the scar on my neck. She also told Diane I work for the FBI. Needless to say, she was hurt I lied to her. And get this, she's the one who called the police to give them the descriptions of Drake, Chazz, and Mark."

"Really?" I asked in disbelief.

"She said she tried to talk to Will about it, but he didn't want to listen."

"Can we trust her?"

Thankfully, she didn't hesitate. "We can. I like Diane. I don't think there's a bad bone in her body."

"I sure hope not because now she knows who you are and I'm assuming me as well."

She nodded. "But that's not all I found out today. I asked Ronnie if I could talk to her girls and she agreed. When I went to the ranch, I told them I was there for an interview. All I did was bullshit with them for a few and asked them about their experiences with Vegas men. They all thought I was new in town, which in all honesty, I kind of am. Anyway, we got on the subject of men who like it rough. Can you guess who their top man is?"

"Drake?"

"Nope, Chazz. And obviously, they lived to tell about it. The only person no one has lived to tell about is Mark."

"Fuck me," I grumbled, holding her face in my hands. "As much as I want to solve this case, I don't want to see you get hurt. If Mark wins you this weekend,

I don't think I can let you go."

   She kissed me gently, pressing her forehead to mine. "You don't have a choice."

CHAPTER 20

AYLEE

"I don't like you doing this," Diane hissed in my ear. I looked over at Jason, his whole body tense. "You're not the only one."

"Why can't you just get warrants to search their homes? Isn't that how it usually works?"

"Not when you're dealing with powerful men. You wouldn't believe how corrupt the system is. People like Jason and I can't be bought. Besides, we don't even have proof that any of them are guilty." The men were on their third round for the night and I knew it was about time for the real game. "I probably need to get back over there and join them," I remarked. Diane pulled me into her arms and I could feel her body shake. "You okay?" I asked, whispering in her ear.

"Only if you are."

I chuckled lightly. "I'll be fine, I promise. I'm not an amateur. I do know how to kick some major ass."

"I'd like to see that," she laughed, pulling away.

Smiling, I grabbed her hands. "Thank you for everything. For the life of me, I don't know why you've been so nice to me."

"You remind me of someone."

"Who?"

Her eyes grew teary. "The daughter I never had. You're beautiful, strong, brave, and selfless to come out here and risk your life for the sake of others. It's rare to find that these days."

"I see the same qualities in you too, Diane."

"Aylee?" Jason called.

I glanced over my shoulder and he nodded toward the table. "It looks like I'm being summoned." William came up behind Diane, holding her shawl. "And I think you're being summoned as well."

Diane quickly looked back at William and then turned to me, speaking low, "Be careful, especially with Mark and Chazz. I don't like what I heard about them today."

"Me neither, but I've dealt with unsavory men before." Squeezing her hands one last time, I let them go and joined the table. "I see you boys don't know how to have fun without me," I teased. Jason stood and pulled a chair out for me. When I sat down, he brushed his fingers down my arms, making me shiver. "Thank you."

"Are you sure you don't mind playing tonight?" Drake asked.

I smiled wide. "Not at all. But since I'm playing for myself, what are the rules?"

Drake glanced around the table. "I'm sure everyone will agree that you have immunity. Since you're the ultimate prize, we'll be the ones offering the money. Is that fair?" he asked, waiting for everyone's answers. One by one, each man nodded their heads. It was the same group as before: Drake, Chazz, Mark, and Jason.

"What happens if I win? Do I get the money and that's it?"

Chazz was the one who answered this time. "Actually, we all agreed beforehand that if you were to win you'd get the money, but you will have to pick someone to fuck tonight."

"So I get to choose? I think I like this game." Jason growled low to where only I could hear and squeezed my thigh under the table. "Let's get started." My only problem was that if I won, who the hell was I going to pick?

The dealer took his place at the table, shuffled the cards and looked straight at me. "Lady's choice."

"My favorite, Texas Hold'em."

He dealt out the first two cards and I was impressed. I had an ace of hearts and a two of hearts. By the time the dealer was ready to throw down the river card, the pot was already to eighty thousand and I was one card away from a flush.

The final card . . . a six of hearts. "All right, gentlemen, it's time to place your bets," the dealer instructed. Blowing out a frustrated sigh, Jason set in another five grand, knowing very well whatever the outcome I wasn't going to pick him.

Mark glanced over at me and then at his cards, throwing in his five and raising fifteen grand. He was mysterious with his dark hair and dark eyes; a very handsome man. However, underneath all of that brooding sexiness he could be harboring a dangerous secret. None of the girls at the ranch had lived long enough to give me the story on their night with the allusive Mark Chamberlain. The rest of the men called, matching his raise.

They turned their cards over first and Jason actually had a straight; I was impressed. Mark had three kings, Chazz had three fours, and Drake had two pair. "It looks like I have you beat, gentlemen," I announced happily, showing my cards.

Jason sat back in his chair. "Well done, firecracker."

"Thank you," I said, picking up the wads of money.

"I think I seriously need to do this for a living."

"No you don't," Drake blurted. I peered over at him, lifting my brows. "Only because you're so good at what you do. I'd hate for you to waste your talent."

"I have plenty of talents, Mr. Blackwell," I said, wishing I could slap the smile off his face.

Chazz slid his chair back. "And some of us would like to see those talents. Which of us do you want to fuck tonight?"

Forcing a smile, I batted my eyelashes and completely turned my back on him. I had three other options and I sure as hell wasn't going to pick Drake again. Jason stared at me – his jaw tight – knowing very well I couldn't choose him.

I walked by Chazz, putting my arm on his shoulder and leaning down to whisper, "I'm going to make you work a little harder for my goods, stud." I nipped his ear and stood, making my way to Mark. Holding out my hand, I said, "Do you accept?"

Chazz slammed his glass on the table. "Dammit!"

I turned to Chazz and gave him a private smile before addressing Mark once again. "Come on, let's get out of here."

"Are you sure this is what you want?"

Did I want to take the risk of getting killed or maimed? No, but I had no choice. He was the one I really needed answers on. "I'm giving you my hand, aren't I?"

He took my hand and stood, glancing around the table. "Meet me out front. I'll get the car." Letting my hand go, he avoided my gaze and turned, stalking off toward the door.

What is his deal? Jason glared at his retreating form, looking just as clueless as I was. Before leaving, I put all of my money in my purse and intentionally dropped some by Jason's feet. "Uh-oh," I said, kneeling on the floor. "Stay close," I whispered.

"I will."

Getting to my feet, I focused on Drake. "Enjoy the rest of your evening, Mr. Blackwell. Thank you for inviting me to join the game."

Lifting his glass, he took a sip. "It's been my pleasure. Be sure to come again next Saturday. I don't think Davies is going to relax until he gets you out of his system."

"I'm looking forward to it." I looked over at Jason one more time and then started toward the door. I didn't like the unknown and Mark was definitely that. The only thing I could dig up on him was that he worked for William, his wife died two years ago in a car accident, and he spent his free time in casinos. Other than that, his life was a mystery; he wasn't in any other activities.

Taking a deep breath, I reached inside my purse and made sure I had everything I needed. My gun was safely tucked away, along with my phone and the serum. I was ready to go. Mark stood by his black SUV, leaning against it with his arms crossed at the chest, with the passenger door wide open. Clutching my purse, I smiled and descended the stone stairs, my heart pounding out of control. I had no clue where he was going to take me, but I had to believe Jason would be right behind.

"Thank you," I murmured, getting into the car. Mark slammed the door and then walked around the front, looking awfully uncomfortable. When he got in, I turned toward him. "Are you okay?"

He huffed. "I sure as hell hope so."

"Do you want to talk about it?"

"You wouldn't understand."

I scoffed. "You'd be surprised, Mr. Chamberlain. Where exactly are you taking me?" We were headed back toward downtown.

"We're going to my condo. I live a few blocks away from the strip."

"I figured you'd live in a hoity-toity mansion like your friends."

He chuckled. "I used to, but since I'm by myself I didn't see the need anymore. I moved out to the strip about a year and a half ago." We pulled into a parking deck attached to another building that was a smaller high rise compared to the other ones around. He pulled out a key card and pushed it inside the slot for the elevator door to open. "This will take us right up to my floor."

"Nice." I walked inside and he pressed the button for the fifth floor, his uneasiness making me nervous. When the elevator opened, he didn't touch me as we made our way down the hall. Once inside, it reminded me of any normal bachelor pad. The furniture was black leather and everything was crisp, masculine. It wasn't like the flowers you'd see all over the living room my uncle had back home at the B&B.

"Would you like something to drink?" he asked, throwing his coat across one of the kitchen chairs. I followed him into the kitchen where he pulled out a couple of beers. "I don't have any of the fancy shit like Blackwell."

I held out my hand for the beer. "Don't get me wrong, I love a good wine, but I've been opening myself up to trying more beers. My favorite is called Baby Maker. It's so good."

His lips drew back in a smile. "Baby Maker? I'll have to try that one."

"You'll love it, trust me," I said, taking a sip of beer.

He nodded toward the couch. "Do you want to have a seat?"

"Sure." I walked around him and did a quick glance around his condo. It looked like there was only one bedroom and a bathroom. Not exactly the place you'd murder and hack someone up. If he was the killer, he hadn't done any of it there. Sitting down, I plastered on a smile and patted the seat beside me. He sat down and tilted his beer back. "I don't think you've spoken more than ten words to me since I met you. Why is that?"

He cleared his throat, avoiding my gaze. "Caught that, huh?"

I nodded and he finally peered over at me, his dark eyes curious. "I just know your job would require you to have more social skills. Not to mention, I can feel how uncomfortable you are."

"You're good, Ms. McFadden. If you want honesty, I chose not to talk to you in hopes of avoiding this exact situation."

"Why?"

"Because I have no desire to fuck you or anyone else for that matter. The guys have been throwing women in my lap for a year. I'm just not interested."

"Oh," I replied, taken aback. That wasn't what I was expecting to hear. "Are you gay?"

I knew he wasn't, not unless he came out after his wife died. In response, he shook his head and laughed. "I'm not gay."

"Then why do you bring women here if you're not interested?"

Guilt was clearly written all over his face, but over what? Why was he so fucking hard to read? Blowing out a heavy sigh, he leaned his head back on the couch.

"I bring them here hoping I get the desire to fuck them. It just never happens, at least not until I met you. Even then, I still don't think I have it in me."

"Me? What makes me different?"

He ran his hands over his face, gaze weary. "You remind me of my wife."

"I didn't think you were married," I lied.

"I *was* married. She died a few years back. The night I saw you I thought I was in the twilight zone. You both have the same red hair and blue eyes. For the longest time, I thought I could move on from her death, but I can't. I'm not ready. The only reason I would have sex with you is because it'd be easy to imagine it was her."

"So you haven't slept with anyone after her death?"

He shook his head. "Wow, I honestly don't know what to say. I've lost my parents, but never someone as close to me as a lover. I can't imagine the pain."

"At first, it was unbearable, and it didn't help that Blackwell and Davies kept trying to get me to fuck other women. I decided then to put on this charade so they stay off my back."

"If you don't sleep with the girls, what do you do with them when you tell them you don't want their services?" Purse in hand, I was ready to grab my gun if need be. He didn't look like he was about to attack, but you never knew. Grief could make you do fucked up things, but I wasn't expecting what came out of his mouth next.

"I give them money for their silence and send them on their way."

"Silence? What do you mean?"

"I give them money to *say* we had sex even though we didn't. That way it gets the guys off my back and it makes them think I'm fucking other women."

"Never would've thought that."

Finishing his beer, he set the bottle down on the table. "Well, there you have it. How much do you want to stay quiet?"

My heart went out to him and I could feel my eyes burning. Hesitantly, I reached over and placed my hand over his. He tensed at first, but then slowly relaxed. "I don't need anything, Mark. As far as anyone's concerned, we had sex tonight and it was mind-blowing. The money isn't important to me. Besides, I already have a purse filled with it."

He turned is hand over in mine and squeezed it before letting it go. "That you do. How about I take you home?"

"That's not necessary. I can find my own way," I insisted, getting to my feet.

He got up and grabbed his keys off the counter. "I'm sure you can, but I'd feel better knowing you got back safely."

"Thank you. Do you mind if I use your restroom

first?"

"Not at all. It's over there," he said, pointing across the room. I hurried over and shut the door, pulling out my phone.

Me: Heading to the hotel. Or at least I think I am.

Jason: What happened?

Me: I'll tell you later. Right now he wants to take me home. Are you close?

Jason: In the parking deck. I'll see you when you get off the elevator.

After putting my phone away, I flushed the toilet and washed my hands before opening the door. "I'm ready to go."

Mark was by the front door and he opened it for me. Sliding past, I waited for him to lock the door and join me by the elevator. "Just so you know, it's not because you're not beautiful," he murmured.

We stepped into the elevator and I smiled. "Your heart's still hurting; I understand that. And thank you for the compliment. At least you didn't call me cute. I hate that."

The elevator door opened and he chortled lightly. "My wife used to say the same thing. When I first met her, I told her she was cute. The look she gave me!" He shook his head and looked as if he was picturing her face.

Opening the door to his SUV, he helped me in. "I

know you're hurting now, but one day it won't be so bad. When that time comes, don't feel guilty about opening your heart again. You deserve to find happiness."

"Maybe one day I will."

CHAPTER 21

AYLEE

Three days had passed since my night with Mark. Jason and I switched hotels the day after and decided to stay at the Bellagio since that was where Drake and his people liked to frequent the most. Diane called first thing Sunday morning to see if I was alright. Even though she woke us up at six in the morning, it was endearing to know she cared.

The only problem I had with Mark's story was that all the girls who'd been sent to him were dead. His story was heartbreaking, but I didn't have the proof to back it up. On the positive side, he let me go and took me home just like he said he would. Not to mention, there weren't any other prostitutes missing.

Putting his arms around my waist from behind, Jason moaned and bit my ear. "Why don't we go out and see the city tonight?"

"Like a date?" I asked, grinning wide.

He turned me around and I melted under his stare. "If that's what you want to call it. We have four more days until I'm sure you'll be paired up with that worthless cocksucker, so I figured we could have some fun to get my mind off of it."

"Your mind? What about mine?"

Lowering his hands to my ass, he squeezed and pushed his arousal into me. "Don't worry, I know how I'm going to keep you occupied."

"First, we need to get something to eat. I'm famished and I need my energy if I'm to keep up with you tonight."

He smacked my ass and pushed me toward my room. "Get ready so we can come back and have some fun. I have a new game I want to play."

"Oh yeah? Does it involve taking off clothes?"

Licking his lips, he lowered them to mine and bit my lip. "Most definitely. And you can't forget touching . . ."

My insides clenched just thinking about it. I kissed him quickly and backed away. "Give me about fifteen minutes and I'll be ready."

I headed toward my old room. The only thing in it was my luggage, since I'd been sleeping in Jason's room. Digging through the bags of clothes Diane gave me, I pulled out the dress she liked so much. It hit above my knee, flaring out at the waist with colorful flowers and a belt. It was actually very pretty. Instead of wearing a shit ton of makeup, I applied a little mascara and lip gloss.

When I left the room, Jason was already dressed in a pair of dress slacks and a polo shirt, holding his phone. He hadn't seen me yet so I approached slowly. "Yes, that would be great. We'll be down in fifteen minutes," he said into the phone before hanging up.

"Fifteen minutes? Where are we going?"

He turned around and his eyes went wide. "Damn, babe. You're so beautiful."

"Thanks. You don't look bad yourself."

"You ready to go? I figured we could eat dinner in the restaurant downstairs. It's actually supposed to be one of the best places to eat in all of Vegas." Holding out his arm, I took it.

"Let's go then."

We walked to the elevators and rode it all the way to the bottom. The lobby was gorgeous with its flower display on the ceiling. I could stare at the colors for hours if I had the time. When we got to the restaurant, it was packed. "How did you even get a reservation?" I asked as he pulled us through the crowd.

He looked back at me and winked. "I have my connections, firecracker."

Luckily enough, we didn't have to wait and were seated at a private table. "Would you care for a cocktail?" the waitress asked.

"I'd like a glass of Riesling, please," I said.

Jason handed her the drink menu. "And I'd like a gin and tonic."

"Sounds good. I'll be right back."

As soon as she sauntered off, Jason reached over for my hands, his expression grim. "Are you ready for Saturday? We're down to our last suspect."

"I know. I can tell you I'm not looking forward to it. I was sure Mark was who we needed."

He nodded. "So was I, but then after what happened the other night I don't think he's our guy. Not after what you told me."

"Which leaves the one I'm dreading the most, Mr. Handsy."

His eyes turned dark. "How do you think I feel? I'm the one having to let you go with him even though deep down I want to rip the bastard in half."

I squeezed his hand. "Don't worry. I'm not going to let him do anything. I'll have you close, plus, I'll have my own kick ass ninja skills. You have yet to see what I can do."

"Maybe you should show me then," he insisted with a smirk.

"I think I will. You just won't know when I'm going

to strike."

He winked. "Don't threaten me with a good time."

The waitress came by with our drinks and we ordered our food. I sipped on my wine, my mind reeling. Sooner or later, these fun evenings with him were going to end. "Jason," I murmured.

"Yeah?"

"Have you thought about what you're going to do when all of this is over?"

He shook his head. "Not really. You?"

"Probably go back to Maine and help out at the B&B when I'm not working in the lab. I just wanted to make sure we don't cut off all ties. I know we'll be thousands of miles away from each other, but I still want to keep in touch. I can't imagine never talking to you again."

I was hoping he'd say something to clarify what we were doing, but he didn't get the chance. The waitress brought our food and set it down, just as we got company. "Well, hello, you two," Chazz announced, sitting beside me. "I thought I saw you both walk in. At first, I didn't recognize you," he said to me.

"Why? Because I'm not dressed like a whore?"

He tilted his head back, bellowing. "That and you actually look like a normal woman without all that shit on your face. You look much sexier like this."

Jason glared at him. "Do you have a point to all of this, Davies? If not, I'd like you to fuck off. We're in the middle of something here."

He lifted his hands in the air. "No need for hostilities. I'm sure if my girl wanted to be fucked by other men, I'd be that way too. Speaking of which, I have a proposition for you," he stated, facing me.

"Let me guess, you want me to play another round this weekend in hopes that you win?"

"Nope."

I glanced quickly at Jason and then back to him. "Then what do you propose?"

"I'm a persistent man, Ms. McFadden. When I want something, I get it. Instead of gambling for you, I'd like to just offer you the money myself. But you're a hard girl to find."

"It's all part of the allure. I'm sure you'd agree. So, how much are we talking?"

His eyes gleamed. "A hundred grand for you and twenty for Avery."

Jason rolled his eyes. "And you think twenty would be enough for me to let her go with you? Have you lost your fucking mind?"

"How much then?" he countered. "Name the price."

Jason narrowed his gaze. "I want fifty. You give me that and you can have her for the night."

"Done," he said happily. "You'll have your fifty grand when I pick her up Friday night." He laughed and ran a finger down my bare arm. "I'm looking forward to it." Jason clutched his steak knife. I had no doubt he'd use it on some part of Chazz's body if I didn't get him out. Thankfully, Chazz got up on his own. "Until then. Enjoy your dinner."

As soon as he left, I breathed a sigh of relief. "What a prick."

Jason let go of his knife and clenched his hand into a fist. "Whether innocent or guilty, no matter what I do, before I leave Vegas I will fuck him up."

"Not unless I do it first."

"Doesn't matter. I *will* break his fucking face."

"I have no doubt."

Leave it to that douchenozzle to ruin what started out being an amazing date. We ate in silence, Jason seething the entire time. "I never would've thought I'd be this helpless in the goddamned case. You're the one doing everything and there's nothing I can do to help."

"You *are* helping, Jason. I couldn't have done all of this without you. You needed me, but now I need you."

"It's getting harder and harder each time to keep my cool. What would you do if the situation was turned and you had to watch me leave with beautiful women who could possibly kill me?"

I ate the last bite of mashed potatoes and set my fork down. "I'd be furious. But it is what it is. These men want me and I have to find out who's killing these girls. We're lucky nobody else has gone missing."

He scoffed. "That's because they all want you."

Taking his hand, I held it tight. "Can we please not talk about this tonight? I want to spend time with you and get to know you, not talk about the case."

"Would you like for me to take your plates out of the way?" the waitress asked.

I let go of Jason's hand and sat back. "You can take mine."

"Sir?"

Jason nodded and handed her his plate. "I'm done. Thank you, it was delicious."

"Would either of you like dessert?"

My eyes lit up and Jason laughed. It was good seeing a smile on his face again. "What do you want, firecracker?"

I looked up at our server. "I would love to have one of the lava cakes. But is there any way to order it for us to pick up later? I want to go out for a walk and then come back. How about two hours from now?"

"Of course. Would you like one too?" she asked Jason.

His smile grew wider. "Why not? Whatever I don't eat, I'm sure she will finish."

"I'll put it in and have it ready for you in two hours. In the meantime, I'll get your check. Have fun on your walk." She sauntered off and came back with our check, which I stole out of Jason's hands.

"What do you think you're doing?"

Closing the booklet, I set it on the table. "Paying. Have you seen the insane amount of cash I have? My uncle's going to freak out when I give him his birthday present."

"Are you going to give him the money?"

"Most of it. He deserves it after putting up with me for the past seventeen years. I never had to pay for anything, not even my first car. It's time I paid him back."

"What was your first car?"

"It was a ninety-three, metallic blue Acura Legend. It was also a manual transmission. Learning on those hilly roads by the B&B almost gave my uncle a heart attack."

"Why does it not surprise me that your first car was a stick?"

"Probably because you know I like things difficult," I laughed. "It was a good car. I drove it until it had over two hundred thousand miles on it. What was yours?"

"It was an old Mazda 626. The paint was even chipping off the hood because it was so old. I begged my parents for a truck, but they made me take that. My sisters got the better deal."

"Oh yeah? How so?"

Standing, he reached for my hand. "Why don't we go for that walk and we can talk as much as you want?"

Holding his hand, he helped me stand. "I'd like that. I've been dying to watch the fountain light show." We walked outside and since it was getting dark, the heat wasn't as bad. There were people everywhere, walking around, laughing, and talking just like us. For a moment, I wanted to pretend everything was normal and I was there on vacation—not risking my life.

"Where were we?" he asked.

"I was inquiring about your sisters. You said they got better cars than you."

"Oh yeah, that's right. I got the old paint chipped car and they got a brand new Nissan Sentra. They did, however, have to share it for awhile. So I guess I can't complain too much."

"I would rather have the beater car than have to share." I laughed.

Letting my hand go, he put his arm around my shoulder. "Yeah, I guess you're right. Anyway, you already know what happened to Braylen. Brooklyn is the feisty one. You and she would get along great."

"Do you ever talk to her?"

"Occasionally. She knows I'm out here working so her incessant phone calls have calmed down a bit. For the longest time, she was all I had."

"I wish I had a sister or even a brother. It would've been nice to not be so lonely over the years. I miss my mother more than anything. I guess that's why I latched onto Diane so easily. She reminds me of her."

"You two have gotten close. She's called you more in the last three days than my mom has in the past three months." We walked over to the rail and it was about time for the light show. He leaned up against the post and pulled me to him, holding tight. "Are you going to miss her when you go home?"

"I'm going to miss a lot of things, you being the main one. I never thought I'd say this, but you've really grown on me."

"Right back at ya, firecracker," he murmured, kissing my head.

"Do you think we'll ever see each other again?" My heart hurt just thinking about it. I couldn't demand anything from him since we hadn't known each other long, but dammit to hell, I wanted to hold onto him as long as I could. He made me feel things I never thought possible. I didn't want to give that up.

He sighed. "I don't know, baby. I just don't know."

About that time, the fountains started to light up and the water shot up in the air. I pulled out of Jason's arms so I could see it, but I really wanted to hide the hurt on my face. Maybe I was expecting too much from him.

Once our two hours were up, we ventured back to

the hotel and picked up our lava cakes. Chocolate could always help mend a hurting heart.

"You ready to play some games tonight?" he asked as we made our way to the room.

I smiled. "Are you?"

He winked, opening the door. "More than ready."

I set my lava cake box down and retreated to my room. "I just need to change. Give me a minute."

"Okay, I'll get the cards ready."

Shutting the door, I opened my bag and got out a pair of shorts, my sports bra, and a fitted T-shirt. I had to be able to move around. I took off my dress and carefully laid it on the bed before joining Jason in the living room.

He was sitting at the table with both lava cakes and a deck of cards. He looked back at me and whistled. "I bet you could put on a potato sack and still look sexy as hell."

"Thanks. What game are we playing? Or better yet, what game have you managed to come up with?"

He shuffled the cards, smirking. "Come over here and find out."

Kneeling down on the other side of the table, I watched him shuffle the cards, wearing nothing but a pair of jeans. I wanted to tell him that he could pull off a potato sack too but I was pretty sure he already knew. Jason Avery was an arrogant ass, but he was mine; at least, for the next few days.

"Give me one sec," I said, getting to my feet. I walked into the kitchen and grabbed a bottle of water out of the refrigerator. "Are you thirsty?"

"Yeah, could you bring me a beer?"

I grabbed him a beer and set it on the edge of the counter, leaving it there while I walked back into the living room. Setting my water on the table, he looked at it and then at my hands. "Where's mine?"

"Oops, I left it on the counter. Sorry."

"Why do I not get the feeling you are?"

I shrugged. Maybe if he told me he was going to miss me, I would've been a little nicer. "I don't know. It was an honest mistake."

"Yeah, right," he mumbled under his breath. As soon as he turned his back on me, I struck low and hard, swiping his feet from under him. He let out an oomph sound when he face planted on the floor.

"To be one of the best around, you sure do drop your guard a lot."

Still lying on the floor, he flipped onto his back so he could face me. "Only around you. I'll know not to make that same mistake again." He tried to snatch my ankle – his hand a blur as it moved – but I jumped back, narrowly escaping. My retreat didn't last long because he was on his feet, ready to attack. "All right, firecracker. Show me what you got."

"Gladly."

We faced off but he attacked first, lunging for my legs. I dodged and slapped him upside the head, only to have him come around and grab me from behind. "You gotta be much faster than that, baby." He grabbed my breasts and squeezed, growling his satisfaction in my ear.

As much as I wanted to stay like that, I couldn't let him beat me. Taking his arm, I twisted and he let go, hissing in pain. I pushed him away. "Not fair, Mr. Avery."

He cracked his neck. "I don't play fair. Now stop wasting time and show me you can fight. I have to know you can handle this."

Clenching my teeth, I attacked and wasn't about to stop. He blocked my punches and kicks, not even attempting to fight back. My muscles burned and my body ached, but I couldn't give up, not until the pain in my chest went away. I wanted to hit him, to smack him over and over until he could give me a fucking answer. Just a simple few words was all I wanted to hear.

Grabbing my waist, he knocked me down to the floor and flipped so he took the hit. We rolled around, him trying to get a hold of my arms and ended up with him on top. I knew I could escape, but I gave up, lying there while my heart and lungs felt like they were going to explode.

"You're not half bad," he said, holding my hands

above my head. His fingers laced with mine and he leaned closer, but I turned my head. "Aylee, what's wrong?" When I wouldn't answer him, he let my hands go and grabbed my face, forcing me to look at him. "What the fuck? Talk to me."

"I don't have anything to say."

Eyes wild, he searched my face. "I can't help you if you don't tell me what's wrong."

I pushed against his chest. "It doesn't matter. You wouldn't understand."

Clutching my wrists, he sat up and peered down at me, his face softening. "You may *think* I don't understand, but I do. You may not be an open book, but I've been around enough to get a good read on you."

"Doubtful. All you know is what positions I like in bed."

"That's bullshit and you know it."

"Do I?"

"How can you say that? You make me out to be this arrogant ass who only wants to fuck you. Have I not made myself perfectly clear with my actions?" He lifted his brows, waiting on my answer, but I couldn't speak. "No comment? Well let me tell you, out of all the missions I've been on, this one is by far the worst. I don't mind being in the line of fire, but watching you head straight into the flames is almost unbearable. I had never been so goddamned afraid and pissed off in my life." His green eyes blazed and it took my breath away.

"Why do you feel that way?"

"Are you seriously going to ask me that? I care about you, Aylee. You asked me earlier what was going to happen when all of this is over and I saw your face when I didn't answer. The answer is this . . . I don't fucking know. I have feelings for you, much deeper than I ever thought possible. I want things to work out between us, but I don't know what's going to happen when we go our separate ways. All I do know is that I'm going to miss you. I'll miss everything about you, even your stubborn ass temper."

Ripping my hands from his grasp, I grabbed him around the neck and pulled him down to my lips.

"I guess that made you happy," he said between kisses.

"Very."

He trailed his lips down my neck and nipped my collarbone. "Then let's see what else makes you happy." Taking my hands, he pulled them away from his face and jerked me to my feet. Lifting me over his shoulders, I squealed when he threw me down on the couch, spreading my legs with his body. "Do you see what you do to me?" he growled, thrusting his body against mine. He was hard and bulging behind his fuck me jeans.

Ripping off my shirt, he threw it and my bra across the room; his mouth everywhere, tasting, biting. When

I tried to unbutton his jeans, he grabbed my hand. "Not yet. There's something I want to do first," he murmured huskily. Sliding back, he pulled my shorts and underwear off, leaving me completely naked. His gaze raked over my body and he moaned in satisfaction. "You know what else would be perfect?"

"What?" I whispered.

Biting his lip, he looked over at the lava cakes and then back to me, his gaze heated. He slid off the couch and unbuttoned his jeans, letting them fall to the floor. I squeezed my legs together trying to quell the ache, but nothing helped. Kneeling down on the floor, he grabbed his spoon and cut his lava cake in half. The chocolate oozed out and he swiped some on his finger, sucking it off while watching me the entire time.

"Do you want some?" he asked. I licked my lips and nodded. He scooped up more chocolate and traced my lips with it. Before I could lick it off, he bit my lip and sucked it off himself.

"That's not fair," I groaned.

Putting his finger in his mouth, he cleaned it off and then kissed me hard, forcing his tongue inside. "You can taste it now, can't you?"

I could and it was fucking heaven. "I want more."

Sliding the plate over, he scooped more chocolate on his finger and traced it all over my nipples and breasts. Once I was covered, he pushed his finger into my mouth and slammed his cock into me at the same time. I cried out and sucked him clean, my body shaking with the force of his body pushing into mine. I was so close to losing control, but he stopped and put a hand on my back and the other on my ass, hauling me up so I straddled his lap.

My body was so wet I slid down his cock with ease, stretching me wide. He ran his tongue over my nipples to lick the chocolate off and bit down, making me scream. I rode him hard, loving the way he grunted in my ear. Grabbing a fistful of my hair, he held on as I clenched down on him, riding out wave after wave of my release. His cock pulsated deep inside, filling me with his warmth. He rubbed my back and I laid my head on his shoulder to catch my breath.

"Are we good now?" he asked, his voice low.

Snickering, I shifted in his lap, his cock still hard inside me. "Nothing will ever beat chocolate and sex. Not to mention, eating chocolate while having sex."

He looked over my shoulder, grinning wide. "We still have another lava cake. You up for another round?"

I bit his lip and nodded. "This time, the chocolate goes on you."

CHAPTER 22

JASON

"How do you know the owner?" Aylee asked. We were on our way to Rushing's Gym and Fitness so we could work out. I needed something to punch instead of Chazz's face when he came to pick her up tonight. I'd been dreading the moment all fucking week.

"He's a good friend and also a UFC Heavyweight Champion. His wife is the owner of K&B Bistro. You remember her, right?"

"Yes, of course. I didn't know you knew so many MMA fighters. You'll need to take me to a fight sometime."

"I'm sure that can be arranged. I actually just worked

a case out here not too long ago for a girl who works here. Her name's Megan. Hopefully, you'll get to meet her."

"What kind of case?"

"Abusive boyfriend turned psycho. But she's alive and well, so that's all that matters."

"I can't imagine. I'd kick anyone's ass who even attempted to lay a hand on me. Anyway, it'll be good to get some exercising in. Lava cakes are doing nothing for my figure."

Looking over at her plump breasts, I bit my lip. "You look sexy as hell. Besides, it'll be good for us to get away from the hotel. All I'm doing there is thinking about you leaving tonight with that cocksucker."

"Do you not think I'm ready?" she asked, concern in her voice.

I pulled into the parking lot and we both got out. "I know you're ready, Aylee. It doesn't change the fact that it's inevitable. I *have* to let you go tonight."

She circled around the car and put her arms around my neck. "But you'll be close by. I won't be alone."

"No, you won't. Now let's go." Taking her hand, I pulled her toward the door. It was late morning and there were a lot of people around. Little did she know, I had a plan cooked up. When we walked inside, Tyler was by the front desk and chuckled when he saw us. He was simply massive, with muscles twice the size of mine. The ladies loved him.

"Well, if it isn't Mr. Armed and Dangerous. What's up, brother?" he announced, holding out his hand. We shook and then he extended his welcome out to Aylee, who smiled and shook back.

"You don't mind letting us workout in your gym today do you?"

He shook his head. "Of course not. Take all the time you need. If you require anything, just let me know."

As soon as he strolled off, I searched for the person I was looking for but he was nowhere to be seen. Aylee flicked my arm, grabbing my attention.

"Do you mind if I disappear to the treadmills? I need to get in a few laps."

I nodded. "I'll be over by the punching bag. I need to hit something."

"Have fun with that," she laughed and took off. I watched her stretch and put in her earphones before pounding away on the treadmill.

"Avery," a voice hissed low.

I glanced over to the doorway leading to the back. When I passed through the door, Tyler stood there with Kyle Andrews, the guy I was looking for earlier. He was big and muscular just like Tyler, but he was the one I needed. His hair was platinum blond and his eyes were two different colors. Given his past with being a douche, I had no doubt he could pull off this plan.

"I can't believe you want me to fuck with your girlfriend," Kyle whispered. He looked out the door at her and shook his head. "And she's a redhead too. She's gonna kick my ass *and* yours."

"Good, that's what I want. This case we're working on is beyond dangerous. She fought me yesterday, and half-assed it. She's strong, but I don't know the extent of her fighting skills. I need to see she can handle herself."

Tyler slapped Kyle on the shoulder. "Don't worry, Avery. Andrews likes being the whipping boy, don't you?"

He grimaced. "Shut the fuck up. I'm doing this to be helpful. How many times can you say I did that for someone?"

Tyler chuckled. "Not many, but you're working on it."

Aylee was about to get off the treadmill. "All right, Andrews, you're up. And don't say I didn't warn you; she's feisty."

As soon as he walked off, Tyler bumped me in the shoulder. "Let's go to my office. We can watch through the window. She won't see us."

I followed him down the hall and once inside his room, I got a clear view of Aylee, wiping her head off with a towel. She glanced around the gym, most likely looking for me, but got distracted when Kyle blocked her path. "I wish I could hear what he's saying."

Tyler snorted. "This is Andrews we're talking about. I'm sure he's saying how he'd like to take her to the back room and fuck her right in the pussy or something crude like that."

"Does that shit actually work for you fighters?"

"Some girls like it dirty. I had my fair share of women before Kacey, who'd fuck me no matter what I said to them."

I shook my head and watched as Aylee tried to walk away from Kyle, her jaw and fists clenched. He kept following her with a goofy grin, running his mouth. Tyler and I watched in anticipation, waiting for her to blow.

"Would she really fight a man who outweighs her by a hundred pounds?"

I snorted. "She'd fight with a brick wall; she's that goddamned stubborn."

"Then she'd fit in perfectly with our crowd. How long do you think you'll be in town?"

"Don't know. Tonight she's investigating our last suspect. He's a fucking douche too. The thought of her going in alone scares the hell out of me. If he's the one we're looking for then our time here'll be short. If he's not, I don't know what we'll do. We can't stay here forever."

He put his hand on my shoulder. "You'll catch them. You're one of Mason's best." That I was, but Aylee was the one doing all the work. She deserved all the credit and then some. "It looks like the shit's about to hit the fan."

Aylee's shouts could be heard through the glass and then out of nowhere her fist flew and connected with Kyle's face. "Holy shit," Tyler and I both said simultaneously. But she was nowhere near done. She hit him again and kicked his legs out from under him. By now, everyone in the gym had gathered around to see the show, their eyes bugging out of their heads. Grabbing him around the neck, she squeezed, her own face turning as red as Kyle's.

"We should probably get out there," Tyler insisted.

"I think so too." We took off down the hall and I raced through the doorway. "Aylee, stop!"

"Fuck that," she growled. "You wouldn't be saying that if you knew what this disgusting pervert said to me."

"What did he say?"

Kyle had his hands on her arms and pried them away so he could breathe. "I told her she could slob my knob and then I'd fuck her in the ass. Chicks love that shit. What's wrong with that?" He winked at me and Tyler and we both burst out laughing.

Aylee didn't find it funny and pushed Kyle away, glaring at me. "You're really going to laugh? Maybe I should take him up on his offer. What would you say then?"

Extending my hand, I helped Kyle up and he slapped me on the shoulder. He turned around and rubbed his neck. "I'd say it wasn't going to happen. I'm a taken man, sweetheart." Then to me, he said, "No need to worry about her, bro. She's ready for any fucker who tries to mess with her."

"Oh my God, this was a setup?" she exclaimed, thundering toward me.

I held up my hands. "I had to see what you would do without me around. You kicked his ass, baby. I'm proud of you."

She pointed an angry finger at me. "Don't call me baby. I knew I shouldn't have gone easy on you in the hotel room."

Kyle chuckled. "What's stopping you now? I think he deserves payback for what he did today. You can fight it off in the ring."

"Uh-oh, do I need to get the gloves out?" Tyler asked, waggling his eyebrows.

Aylee lifted her chin defiantly in the air. "Yes." She brushed past me with a devilish smile on her face. She was ready to fight and I was going to give her one.

CHAPTER 23

AYLEE

"I have to admit, seeing you in the ring was a fucking turn on," Jason hollered from the living room.

Giggling, I finished up my makeup and joined him. "So that's why you attacked me as soon as we got back."

"Couldn't help it." He looked me up and down and sighed. "You look stunning by the way."

"Thanks," I replied, glancing down at my silky, blue dress.

"Do you have everything you need?"

I patted my purse. "Gun is safely tucked away and I have two serums, just to be on the safe side. The others are in my suitcase."

He walked up to me and held my face in his hands. "I know you're sick of me saying this, but be careful."

I breathed him in. "I will." A knock sounded on the door and he growled low in his chest. "I'll get it so you don't try to kill him." Taking a deep breath, I let him go and started for the door. However, it wasn't just Chazz standing there when I opened it.

"Hello, beautiful," he greeted.

I looked over at the girl standing next to him and recognized her as one of Madame Chatfield's. She was shorter than me with long, brown hair and bright blue eyes, dressed in a short silver dress that barely covered her backside. "I know you," she said with a big smile. "I met you the other day, didn't I?" She held out her hand.

I shook it and let go. "Angelica, right?"

Jason came up behind me. "What's going on?"

Angelica walked past me and clutched his arm. "You were right, he is handsome," she said, beaming at Chazz.

I glanced up at Jason, trying my best not to look panicked or pissed. I didn't like her touching him and I sure as hell didn't like Chazz bringing her.

"Sorry, love, but I'm not interested," Jason claimed, sliding his arm out of her hold.

"She's part of the deal, Avery," Chazz explained. "I didn't want you to be a sore loser, so I hired Angelica here to be your date for the evening. If you turn her down, the deal's off. Make your choice."

Jason's eyes darkened menacingly and the room felt icy. Chazz could sense it and met Jason's stare, provoking him. "The deal's off. You're not going to tell me who to fuck and when. And you're sure as hell not going to have Aylee."

Angelica slid out the door and Jason slammed it, only to be stopped by Chazz's foot. "First of all, I don't give a shit what you think. I only care about Aylee. I say we leave it up to her." He pulled out two large envelopes that I knew were filled with money. Jason didn't want me to go, but I had to. It could be my only chance to see if he was guilty. Not to mention, he had Angelica with him. If he didn't take me, it might be her.

Jason gripped the side of my waist. "You can't go," he hissed low.

Taking his hand, I pulled him farther into the room while Chazz and Angelica watched from the doorway. "I don't have a choice. I have to go. I can't let Angelica stay with him. If something were to happen to her I'd never forgive myself."

His fingers dug into my arms, his green eyes wild. "You don't get it. I won't be able to follow you."

"Yes, you will. She can have a date with one of the serums. Once you've slipped her the drug and her eyes close, make sure to verbalize what you did to her. She'll wake up happy and satisfied."

Huffing, he closed his eyes. "Fuck me. Stall as long as you can so I can catch up. I'm going to kill that fucker if he hurts you."

"I'm waiting," Chazz warned.

I rolled my eyes and Jason turned to him. "Keep your dick in your pants, man."

I squeezed his hands. "I'm ready for this. You know I am." Turning, I stalked over to Chazz, taking the envelopes to make sure the money was in them. The transaction made me feel like a prostitute, but I wasn't about to not take it from the bastard.

Chazz waved at Jason and nudged Angelica inside. "You two have a good night. I know I will." He shut the door so fast I couldn't get one last look at Jason. Putting his arm around my waist, I couldn't help but snort in disgust.

"You could have been a little more polite. I'm not sure I want to fuck someone with no manners."

"Keep it up, sweetheart. Feisty women are my favorite. You're only turning me on more. Frankly, I don't see what's so bad about me. I'm good looking and I can fuck all night. Isn't that what you ladies want?"

"Those are good qualities, but it helps to not be a dick."

"But I am one. You're just going to have to get the fuck over it."

We'll see about that. We got in the elevator and he

pushed me against the wall, groping my breasts and slobbering on my neck. It took all I had not to knee him in the balls.

"I'll take care of you tonight. Once I'm done with you, you're going to wish you were with me and not that wannabe."

"You honestly think you can make me forget him?"

He traced my nipples with his fingers and pushed his arousal into my leg. "No, but I can make sure he forgets you. By the time I'm done, you won't be able to walk for a week. He'll have no use for you then."

At least he planned on bringing me back. Or was that his game, toy with his prey before going in for the grand finale? One thing I'd come to realize was that serial killers were extremely fucked up in the head. There was no rhyme or reason for the things they did.

The doors opened and Chazz stepped away, but put his arm around my waist. "If you despise me so much, why did you agree to come with me tonight?"

"From the way you acted before, I figured it was the only way to get you off my back. You're a persistent bastard."

Tilting his head back, he bellowed. "That I am. But if you're a good fuck, I might not be able to leave you alone."

"In that case, I might consider a different profession."

All he did was laugh the whole way out to his car.

"I have to say, you're not like the others. I do believe you're what I've been looking for."

I'm sure I was. And what do you know, he drove an expensive, flashy sports car. *Surprise, surprise.* I opened the door and got in, making sure to keep my purse close. I really hoped Jason had enough time to get rid of Angelica. If not, I was going to be on my own. "Where do you live?" I asked.

He put the car in gear and sped us out of the parking lot. "About twenty minutes from here." We drove away from the city and I couldn't help but think about Jason and what he was doing. The thought of him being alone with another woman infuriated me. Now I knew what it felt like to be him when he had to watch me leave with different men.

"All right, we're here," he said, pulling us into a swanky neighborhood. After a few more turns, we had arrived. It was a three story mansion with a five car garage. Even if I had the money to afford a place like that, I wouldn't buy it. Instead of parking in the garage, he pulled in front of the house and shut off the car. "You ready?"

"I guess I have to be." I made sure to assess everything about my surroundings. There were other houses around, but there was a good three hundred feet between them. Chazz unlocked the door and pushed it open. I walked inside and my muscles tensed, knowing very well that when he shut the door I was going to be locked away from everyone else. The door slammed behind me and he sighed.

"Home sweet home. Do you like it? I had it built a year ago."

"It's nice."

"Do you want me to show you around?"

Heart racing, I nodded and forced a smile. He started off in the living room and walked through the kitchen. As soon as he turned his back to me, I made sure I had easy access to my gun and the serum. Next, we walked back through the living room and to the stairs. "I'm surprised you don't have a fancy wine cellar. Wine's my favorite."

He started up the stairs and stopped, smirking devilishly at me over his shoulder. "I have a basement, but I didn't think you'd be interested in seeing that just yet."

"Why is that?" I asked slowly.

Chuckling, he continued up the stairs. "Let's just say it's where I like to have fun. I might need to warm you up first before we go down there."

He showed me the rest of the house, including his bedroom which was where we ended up. "Do you have anything to drink?" I asked. He walked over to the mini bar in the corner of his room and lifted a fancy glass bottle filled half-way with an amber liquid.

"Scotch?"

"Sure."

He poured a little in two different glasses and handed me one while he took a sip of the other. All I needed was for him to step away so I could squirt the serum into his drink. Unfortunately, it didn't look like that was going to happen; he watched me like a hawk. I took a sip of the scotch and felt the burn go down my throat. That was when the idea hit. Turning my back to him, I glanced up at his walls and pointed at the paintings.

"Those are very interesting. What made you choose them?" He walked toward me, but I kept my back to him and continued my stroll around his room. Slipping my hand into my purse, I pulled out one of the syringes and expelled the contents in my own drink, quickly sticking the vial back in my purse. I had a plan and I hoped to hell it worked. If not, I only had one dose left. I stopped so he could join me and looked up at the last painting.

"To be honest, I didn't choose them; my interior designer did. She thought they matched my personality."

Snorting, I nodded up to it. "I'd say she hit the nail on the head."

"Why is that?"

"Let's see . . . they're all black, white, and gray. Abstract. It also shows a dark and wild side. Not too sure if I like that combination."

"You're about to see it, sweetheart. Don't worry, I

think you'll like it once I break you in." Taking my arm, he pulled me out the door and back down the stairs toward the kitchen. There were no extra doors that could possibly lead to a basement. However, that didn't mean there weren't any. What appeared to be just a wall of cabinets, turned into a large door that swung open, revealing a set of stairs leading into the darkness below.

He dragged me along, but I planted my feet into the floor. "I don't think I'm going to enjoy what's down there."

"Are you scared? Out of all the girls I've fucked, you were the last one I'd suspect to be scared."

"I'm not scared. I just don't like surprises."

"Once you see what's down here, you won't be surprised anymore. It's all laid out for you."

Taking a deep breath, I took a step forward and let him guide me down the stairs. It was dark, but there was a red light glowing from deep within. I felt like I was in a horror movie sneaking into a house where the killer awaited my arrival. But curiosity killed the cat. Once I stepped off the last stair, I had to blink my eyes a few times to comprehend what I was seeing. "Oh my God."

Chazz turned on another red light, highlighting the bed in the corner of the room. There weren't axes, knives, or anything that could be used to mutilate someone's body, but there sure as hell were sexual torture devices, a flogger being the first thing I saw. It wasn't the room of doom I was expecting, but a sadist's room of pleasure. Chazz picked up the flogger and slapped it on the red, silky bed sheets. "I think your ass will look perfect being the same shade as your hair."

"You want to whip me?" I asked incredulously.

Setting his glass of scotch down, he unbuttoned his shirt and tossed it across the room. "Why not? Has Avery never punished you before?"

"Not like that."

"You're both missing out then. It's pleasurable, heightens the senses."

"For you maybe," I scoffed.

Setting the flogger down, he beckoned me toward the table of toys. Not only was there a flogger, but there was a whip, handcuffs, rope, a couple of different sized dildos and a few other things I could only imagine what were used for. "Do I use the dildos on you?"

He picked one up and handed it to me. "It's for me to watch you use. Surely you've pleasured yourself before?"

"I'm a woman, Mr. Davies. I'm sure you can figure that out."

"Then get on the bed and show me."

I turned and walked over to his drink, quickly switching it with mine before I handed it to him. "I need a drink first."

He held his glass and brought it to his lips. "You must be new at this. The women I bring here aren't usually so . . . nervous."

"I'm not nervous. I just need a fucking drink," I growled. He watched me until I downed all of mine, then he finally did as well. Breathing a sigh of relief, I set my glass down. The effects of the scotch began to make me feel fuzzy.

Chazz grabbed my arm and turned me around, his breath hot by my ear. "I want this dress off now." Sliding the straps down my shoulders, he ripped the rest of it off my body and he bent me over, pushing my chest onto the bed. His belt clanked as he undid it, dropping his pants to the floor. I had about four minutes left for the serum to knock him out, but his sexual tendencies had been heightened.

"I thought you wanted me to use the dildo?" I asked hastily. Grabbing me by the waist, he held me in place with one hand, but he swayed on his knees. His cock was between my legs and he trembled, moaning as his hands glided across my body. *Three minutes.*

"Your skin . . . feels so . . . so fucking good," he slurred. I stood up and leaned against him, rubbing my back against his chest. His fingers dug into my hips and I yelped, grimacing in pain as his body jerked. I was going to have half moon scratches on my skin after that. Pushing his cock between my legs, it didn't take long for him to come all over the bed. *Two minutes*. "Holy fuck, what are you doing to me?" He leaned against me, his body growing heavy.

I rolled out from under him and watched him fall face first into his own jizz. Slapping a hand over my mouth, I tried to silence my laughs. He was going to hate me after tonight. "I guess it's a good thing I don't care."

He moaned and just laid there, completely worthless. After quickly slipping on what was left of my dress, I checked my phone, thankful Jason had found me. My torn dress was barely covering my body and there was no way I was going to walk the streets at night like that. Not to mention, I was going to have to deal with Jason's wrath once he saw me.

Jason: I'm here.

Me: I wish I wasn't. Chazz is clean. Well, maybe not at the moment.

Jason: ?

Me: Tell you soon. Be out in 10 minutes.

Grabbing the rope off the table, I wrapped it around Chazz's wrists and tied him to the bed posts. He moaned and started thrusting his hips into the bed. "Let's see how you like being the tortured one, Mr. Davies. From now on, I bet you're going to love getting your ass flogged."

I left the ropes semi-loose so he could get out on

his own when he woke up. I would love to see his face when that happened, all covered in his dried-up semen. Taking the flogger, I traced it over his back and he shivered. It was strange to see the effects the serum had on different people. In the lab, I didn't excite my hosts so it was simply watching them pass out and recording the lengths of time and their vitals.

"How about we make *your* ass the same color of my hair? That way it's you who won't be able to walk for a week." Lifting the flogger high, I slapped it across his backside and he groaned. Little red welts appeared on his skin and I smiled. "You want one more?" When he didn't answer, I did it anyway, only harder. Now that his ass was red, my work was done.

However, my victory was short lived. There was nothing in Chazz's basement that would suggest he was a killer. We were back to round one. Before going up the stairs, I glanced at him one more time and sighed. My search wasn't over, but now I had no clue what to do. Tiptoeing up the stairs, I pulled out my phone.

Me: Coming out.

Jason: I'll come get you.

I wasn't ready to explain to him why my dress looked like a bear slashed through it, but hopefully, I could get him away before he tried to kill Chazz. Finding one of his coats, I slipped it over my tattered dress before walking out the door.

Jason pulled in just as I came out of the house. He got out of the car and raced up to me. "Are you okay? Why are you wearing that?"

"I was cold. Let's just get out of here." He opened the car door for me and rushed around to his side. "What happened with Angelica?"

"She's passed out in my bed. As soon as you left, I went straight to your room and put some serum in her wine. I don't think I said more than two words to her the entire time." The second he sped us out of the driveway, I breathed a sigh of relief. I wanted him as far away from Chazz as possible. "Now tell me what happened," he demanded.

I shrugged. "I don't think Chazz is who we're looking for. He took me for a tour of the house before anything ever happened."

He grimaced. "I was wondering what took so long."

"Everything was pretty normal until we got to his basement."

His head snapped my way. "Basement? What the fuck was in there?"

"A sadist's dream come true."

"You can't be serious. Are we talking whips, chains, and all that bullshit?"

I nodded. "He gets his jollies by using them."

His anger filled the car, his knuckles turning white as he gripped the steering wheel. "He didn't use any of that on you, did he?"

"On the contrary, now he'll be the one needing a rubber donut to sit down."

Thankfully, that brought a smile to his lips. "No, you didn't."

"Oh, yes I did. He's going to be uber pissed when he wakes up."

"Good. Serves the fucker right. I was thinking we should call Chatfield and get her to pick up her girl. That way we can get her out of the way."

"Good idea. I can also give her the news we're back at square one. I have no clue who the killer is."

"We'll figure it out. It could still be one of them. The victims weren't knowingly with any of them the nights they died. We just have to wait and see who comes after you next, if anyone."

"Ryan's not going to like this. We probably need to get in touch with him in the morning."

Jason tucked my hair behind my ear and I leaned into his touch. "We'll take it one step at a time, baby. It looks like you've had enough for one night."

I was disappointed, but shamefully, also relieved. Solving the case meant we were done, that I had to leave Jason. I wasn't ready for that, but I also had a duty. Duty had to come first.

CHAPTER 24

AYLEE

"Thank you for calling me," Ronnie said, coming through the door.

"You're welcome. I called you as soon as I was done with Chazz." Jason and I had just walked in ourselves. I hadn't even had time to change clothes. Luckily, she brought a buff young man to help—Thor, a male escort. Jason led him to the bedroom and he came out carrying Angelica in his strong arms.

Ronnie sighed and nodded toward the door. "Take her to the car, please. I'll be down in a minute." As soon as he left and the door shut, she faced me. "What happened? Do you know who the killer is?"

I shook my head. "I haven't been able to find

anything on anyone. We're not going to give up though. Did you know Angelica was going with Chazz tonight?"

"No, she failed to tell me. You might have just saved her life. I wish I knew how to keep my girls safe."

"Like you said before, you can't. It's a dangerous profession, just like my job. It's something you can't control."

Her lips pulled back in a sad smile. "You're right. I guess I shouldn't get attached. Okay, I'll keep in touch if I hear anything or if any of my girls go missing." She started for the door and walked out, leaving me alone with Jason.

"You ready to call it a night, babe?" he asked softly.

"Sure, just let me get some clothes out of my room. Do you mind getting me a bottle of water? I feel a little dehydrated."

Narrowing his eyes, he raked them up and down my body. "You sure you're okay?"

"I'm fine," I replied, plastering on a fake smile. "Really."

I walked to my room and rushed to my suitcase to find something to wear. Ripping off the jacket, I glanced quickly at my tattered dress and started to take it off, only to stop when I felt a pair of eyes on my body. In the mirror, Jason glared at me, his fists clenched.

Turning around, I slowly approached. "I can explain."

"No need," he growled. "I'll take care of it myself." Storming off, he grabbed his keys and headed for the door.

"Jason, *stop*. Where are you going?"

"To kill that motherfucker! He's not going to get away with this." He reached for the door handle, but I barreled into him and stood in his way.

"He didn't hurt me," I cried.

His nostrils flared, especially when he looked at my arms. "What do you call this?" he shouted, pointing at my wrists. There were already bruises showing up from where Chazz held onto me. Swallowing hard, I closed my eyes and then opened them slowly.

"Okay, so maybe he hurt me a little, but it's not as bad as it looks. Trust me, if he'd gotten his dick anywhere near my orifices I was going to cut the fucking thing off."

"It doesn't matter! He left marks on you!" His eyes blazed and it was frightening. I'd never seen him look that way. "Where else did he hurt you?"

"Nowhere."

He stepped back as if I'd slapped him. "After everything we've been through . . . you're going to fucking lie to me? Tell me the fucking truth!"

Frozen, I stood there staring into his tormented green gaze. It was in that moment I realized I loved him. Instead of waiting on me to show him, he lowered my tattered dress to the floor and I let him. His fingers brushed across my collarbone on down to my breasts and my stomach. A murderous growl escaped his lips when he found the marks on my hips. Reluctantly, I looked down at the damage and closed my eyes. The half moon crescents were deep red and turning purple. Just a simple touch from him made me balk in pain.

"Goddamn, son of a bitch," he yelled. Storming away, he punched a hole in the wall and ran a hand through his hair. "What the hell am I supposed to do? Just let him get away with hurting you?"

"Jason, I knew there was a chance I'd get hurt doing this, maybe even killed. It's the risk we take. There's nothing you can do."

"Like hell there's not. The next time I see him, I don't give a shit where we are, or what's going on. I *will* fuck him up."

Slowly, I walked over to him and I placed my hands on his face. "I paid him back for what he did to me. I flogged him pretty good. So don't think for a second I let him get away with putting his hands on me."

Sighing, he lowered his head. "It's not the same."

"Why? Why is it not the same?"

Lifting his head, he looked down at my lips and kissed me. "Because *I'm* the one who needs to protect *you*, to keep you safe. It's in my blood."

"Is that it? You just want to keep me safe?"

He brushed a finger down my cheek. "Well, there's

that and also one other thing."

"What?"

Taking my face in his hands, he stared into my eyes. "I'm falling in love with you."

I clutched my chest, then jumped into his arms. "I thought I'd never hear you say those words. I'm falling for you too. So much it hurts." He kissed me hard, opening me with his tongue. I wrapped my legs around his waist and he carried me into the bedroom, never taking his mouth from mine. "Make love to me, Jason."

Gently laying me on the bed, he covered me with his body. "Are you sure that's what you want after tonight? I don't want to hurt you."

"You won't. I trust you."

CHAPTER 25

AYLEE

The next morning, I woke up to an empty bed and panicked. "Jason?" There was no sound. I jumped out of bed and slipped on my bathrobe, rushing into the living room. "Jason?" He wasn't in his room either. "Fuck me."

"Gladly, but you'll have to wait until after breakfast."

Jerking around, I watched as Jason came through the door, carrying two cups of coffee and a bag. "What the hell? Why didn't you tell me you were going for breakfast? You had me worried."

He set our stuff down on the counter and I joined him. "You mean you were worried because you thought I'd gone after Davies?"

I bit my lip. "It crossed my mind."

Opening the bag, he pulled out two apple pastries and slid me one. "I'm going after him and nothing's going to stop me, not even you. I just don't want him drugged out of his mind when I do. It's important he remembers my lesson."

I just wished he could see that leaving Chazz face down in his own fluids and a flogged ass was payback enough. The humiliation alone was retribution. "Have you talked to Ryan yet?" I asked nervously. I wasn't looking forward to telling him we didn't have a single shred of evidence from anyone.

He took a bite of his pastry and nodded. "He's coming to see us today. I didn't go into details, but I'm sure he got the hint."

"What do you think he'll say?"

"I don't know, but we'll find out in an hour when he gets here."

I finished my pastry, then hurried off to take a shower while he stayed in the kitchen and worked. After getting dressed, I watched Jason from the doorway to my room, his forehead all scrunched in concentration. The stubble on his face had grown thicker; I liked it that way, even though I knew he hadn't shaved because he was stressed. It made me wonder what things would be like between us if we weren't here for work, if we could just be ourselves.

My phone rang and I jumped, drawing Jason's attention. His muscles relaxed and he smiled. "I knew you were watching me, firecracker."

"It's kind of hard not to. Give me one sec." I hurried over to my phone and my heart leapt when I saw my uncle's name. "Uncle G," I answered excitedly. His name was Gary, but uncle G was what I had called him ever since I was little and it stuck over the years.

"Hey, peanut. Vegas treating you well?"

"Somewhat. It's been a trying case."

"No leads?"

"We've had plenty, but they all ran into dead ends. Hopefully, we'll figure it out soon."

"How's it going working with that other agent? I know you were worried about his reaction."

I snorted. "It was hard at first, but now it's going good. We haven't killed each other yet."

He chuckled. "I'm just glad to hear you're safe. I kept waiting on you to call and when you hadn't, I started to get worried. You can't do that to your old man."

It warmed my heart to hear him say that. "I know, and I'll do much better from here on out. Did Adrian stop by to see you?"

"He did and he left you a present along with a letter. I think he's hoping you'll visit him in New York."

"Yeah, that's what he said when he called."

"Are you going to?" he asked.

Sighing, I sat down on the bed. "I honestly don't know. The last thing I want to do is give him the wrong impression."

"What's changed? He's a good man and he'll take care of you."

Jason stood in my doorway, leaning against the frame. "Oh I know he would, but I've moved on. My feelings just aren't the same as they used to be."

"I see. Well, you take care out there. I know you have more important things to do than talk to me. Be safe and I'll see you soon. Love you, peanut."

I smiled. "I love you too."

Jason walked in and sat beside me. "What all did your uncle say?"

I looked down at my phone and grinned. "Just scolded me for not calling him. He wanted to make sure I was okay."

"It sounded like a little more than that. I heard you mention your ex's name."

Taking his hand, I clasped it with mine. "Adrian and my uncle grew close over the years. He was asking if we were getting back together."

He squeezed my hand. "I see. And when all of this is over . . . are you going to?"

A knock sounded on the door before I could answer. "Ryan's here. I guess we should get that."

He stared at me, then let go my hand. I followed him

out of my room and leaned against the wall while he opened the door. Ryan walked in, wearing a baseball cap, jeans and a T-shirt. It was strange seeing the Chief of Police in normal clothes.

"Good morning," he announced. Jason shut the door and we followed Ryan to the living room where he sat down in one of the chairs. Jason and I sat across from him on the couch, waiting. He glanced back and forth at us, his face full of uncertainty. "I'm assuming from the phone call this morning that you have nothing. What do you think we should do at this point?"

Jason looked at me and then back to him. "I think we need to hold out a little longer. The girls didn't go missing on the nights they were with the suspects. I was looking at the timeline and the dates Aylee was able to get from Chatfield. The murders range anywhere from two days to two weeks after their interactions with them. The killer went after them on nights they weren't accounted for. I'm assuming that's what they'll try to do with Aylee. Or worse, it could be someone completely different."

"Someone we'd least expect," I added. It was highly possible and the thought terrified me. I'd never gone into a case not knowing exactly who I was looking for.

Ryan let out a heavy sigh. "I will tell you one thing of interest. I've been doing my own digging and found something this morning."

"What?" Jason prompted.

He leaned forward. "I found out who's been bribing the news stations to keep quiet about the missing women."

Now it was my turn to ask, "Who?"

"Drake Blackwell."

CHAPTER 26

AYLEE

One Week Later

We were heading to William Randall's house for a celebratory dinner. Mark had procured him another team to own and apparently that team was huge. Diane had called to make sure I was coming and I hadn't wanted to let her down. Besides, Drake was going to be there, and unfortunately, so was Chazz. A week wasn't a long enough time to cool Jason's temper.

There were people everywhere when we walked in, and the first person I saw was Mark, surrounded by a group of people. He acknowledged Jason with a nod and threw a small smile my way.

"Don't know if I like him smiling at you," Jason grumbled under his breath.

"I remind him of his dead wife. My heart hurts for him."

Jason put his arm around me and steered me in another direction. "In that case, I'm keeping you away from him. Don't need him imagining that you're her."

Our first stop was the parlor where Diane was trying to herd everyone into the dining room. When she saw me, she smiled and rushed over, looking beautiful in her gold toned dress. "I hope you're hungry. I had the chefs make broccoli and cheese quiche. It doesn't really go with the menu, but William didn't notice. He's too ecstatic over this new team."

"Is everyone here?" I asked.

She nodded. "Including Mr. Davies who seems a little uptight. You never told me what happened between you two."

I whispered in her ear, "I gave him a bit of his own medicine. I'll spare you the details."

When we got into the formal dining room, the table was large enough to fit twenty-two people. Diane ushered me toward the end where she took a seat and I took the one beside her. Looking down the table, I caught Chazz's gaze at the far end. He glared at me, but I quickly averted my stare, smiling wide.

Once everyone was seated, William was on my opposite side with Mark beside him and Drake just a few seats down, sitting beside his wife. As soon as he was alone, I was going to make my move.

Dinner ended up being four courses and it took two hours to get through it all. William and Jason conversed while I focused my attention on Diane. "Veronica told me none of her girls have been approached by anyone this week. That's a good sign."

I finished my last bite of chocolate cake and leaned closer. "That's true, but it also puts a damper on the investigation. I need someone to make a move. That's why I'm going to corner Drake tonight. When the time comes, can you make sure Georgia is occupied?"

She snorted and glanced over at the middle-aged beauty. "That should be easy. She doesn't particularly stick to her husband's side at these events. Personally, I don't even know why they're married."

Once dinner was over, everyone got up and milled about to different parts of the house. Jason and I kept our eyes on Drake and as soon as he separated from his wife, I went on the hunt. "Stick close to him and I'll make sure his wife doesn't stray," Jason whispered.

"How do you plan on doing that? Besides, I have Diane looking out for her."

"Diane can only do so much. But Mrs. Blackwell is a full-on cougar. She couldn't keep her greedy eyes off me at dinner."

"Great! Now I have to worry about *you* getting attacked. She better keep her claws to herself." Georgia was on the move so we parted ways. The house was enormous, with so many different rooms to explore. Drake disappeared around a corner, entering a room at the end of a hall and shutting the door. By the sounds of it, he was using the bathroom. Not exactly what I called a romantic situation, but I had no other choice.

Leaning against the wall, I waited for him to emerge. When the door opened, I stepped forward. "There you are," I murmured huskily.

His eyes widened, but then he bit his lip, smiling. "What can I do for you?"

"You can give me a good time again. You up for that?"

Stepping closer, he brushed a finger down my neck. "I've been waiting on you to come back to me. Tired of us playing for you?"

"A little. I don't want to take a chance on one of the others winning. What do you say we forget the poker game and make our own plans? I don't want Jason to know about this. It'll be our secret."

He moaned and licked his lips. "I love secrets. How about next Wednesday night? My week is pretty hectic, but I can probably get away then."

"Where?"

"I have a second house not too far away. My wife didn't like it so I bought our current house. Be ready around six. I'll text you and tell you where we can meet."

I gave him my number and he entered it into his phone. "See you then. I look forward to it." He waltzed off and grinned back at me before turning the corner. I pulled out my phone and texted Jason.

Me: Done.

Jason: Where you at? I can't find Davies.

I was about to reply when a hand grabbed my wrist and I was shoved into one of the bedrooms. It was dark and I couldn't see, but I knew who it was. I recognized the smell of his cologne. "Care to turn on the light, Mr. Davies? Or are you afraid to look at me?"

The light shone bright and I squinted. He locked the door and stalked toward me. "I'm not afraid to look at you, whore. I'm here to warn you. If you so much as tell anyone what happened that night . . ."

"You'll what exactly? I'm not scared of you."

He got up in my face and stared me down, his expression hard. "You should be."

"Well, I'm not, so get the fuck out of my way."

"I'll get out of your way when I feel like it."

"No, you'll do it now," a voice growled from behind. Chazz jerked around, pulling my arm with him. I hissed in pain and that pushed Jason over the edge. With a murderous glare, he shut the door quietly and locked it. "Let her go," he demanded.

Chazz released his grip on my arm and stepped to the side. "What is it about this whore that has everyone so hard up? You must be one whipped pussy to keep crawling back to her after she's fucked half the men in Vegas."

Jason didn't waste any time, punching him square in the jaw. But he didn't stop there. Next, he kicked him in the ribs and slammed against the wall, knocking over the trinkets from the dresser. It was loud and I was sure any moment the door would burst open. Grabbing Chazz around the neck, he squeezed. "You don't know the first goddamned thing going on here. Too bad I know . . . you're the one who woke up with a red ass, almost drowning in your own jizz. How did it taste by the way?"

"Fuck you," he choked out.

Jason squeezed harder, slamming Chazz's face onto the dresser. "You need to learn some respect. I saw the marks you left on her body and if it was up to me you'd be dead right now. If you ever touch her again, I'll rip your goddamn head off. You got that?" When Chazz didn't answer, he smashed his face into the dresser again; his face was turning blue. "Answer me!"

"I . . . got . . . it."

Jason tossed him to the floor and stepped on his hand when he walked past. "Let's get the hell out of here."

"How did you know where I was?"

Jaw tensing, he looked down at Chazz and then at

me. "I just did. Now let's go before I do something I'll regret." He unlocked the door, and surprisingly, there wasn't anyone standing around in the hallway. Holding my hand, Jason squeezed it tight and he didn't let go until we got outside and into his car. The farther away we got, the more he seemed to calm down. "Do you think I got my point across?"

"I'd say so. I have to admit, you were sexy as hell kicking his ass."

His lips pulled up into a smirk. "Oh yeah? Did my ninja skills turn you on?"

"I don't know, you tell me." I grabbed his hand and slid it up my dress, rubbing his fingers along my wet opening.

His eyes widened as he looked down to my bared pussy. I grinned and brought his fingers up to my mouth, sucking them clean. Leaning over, I unbuttoned his pants, freeing his cock. It jumped in my hands and hardened as I massaged him.

"What are you doing to me, firecracker?" he moaned, gripping the wheel in his strong grasp.

I leaned over and bit his ear. "I've tasted me," I sucked his lobe between my teeth, "and now I need to taste you, Mr. Avery. Drive safe and let me do all the work."

CHAPTER 27

JASON

For the past few days, sleep was non-existent. I could feel the end drawing near and I didn't like it. Something was off, but I couldn't put my finger on it. It didn't help that I couldn't find a goddamned thing on Drake's *other* house. Not even the Las Vegas PD knew anything about it. Another fucking dead end.

"When do you think he'll text you?" I asked. It was Wednesday afternoon, the day Drake wanted to meet with Aylee. I was on edge.

Shrugging, she slid me a bottle of water and tossed an orange slice into her mouth. "I'm not sure. What I want to know is why can't we find this extra house of his? This could be the place the victims were taken to."

"I know and I can't find shit on it. When Blackwell calls you, I'll get Ryan to get a group of men together. If he takes you to that house, I want to make sure we have the manpower to get you out unharmed."

Leaning over the counter, she shut my laptop and smiled. "I have no doubt you could storm the castle all by yourself."

I sighed. "I know, but you're the one who'll be inside. My only concern is for you."

For the rest of the morning and afternoon, we sat around the hotel mentally preparing for the unknown. Aylee was set, but I was nowhere near ready to let her go. This time was different. When her phone went off, we both froze. She walked over to it and sighed when she read the text.

"He cancelled." She threw her phone to me and I read it.

Drake: Family emergency. Raincheck?

I typed in 'sure' and sent it. Now we were back to the waiting game. "Why does it feel like every time we get close, something pulls us back?"

She joined me on the couch. "I'm just ready to get this shit over with."

So was I.

Two days had passed with no word from Drake. The last thing I was going to do was sit around on my ass and wait for him to make a move. Instead, I was going to take Aylee out for the night, hopefully to relieve some stress.

"Where are we going?" she asked.

Smiling, I pulled us into the parking lot of the Labyrinth. "Have you ever heard of this place?"

She pursed her lips and then nodded. "Yeah . . . wasn't the owner of this place investigated a couple years ago for murder, but turned out to be innocent? It was all over the news."

"He's a good man." We both got out and I put my arm around her as we headed toward the door. Her red hair was pulled up with several of her curls hanging down, framing her heart-shaped face. She was wearing a denim skirt and white top that looked sexy as hell. I loved seeing the real Aylee, the one who could joke around and have fun . . . the one I was in love with.

"What exactly are we doing here?" she asked.

"We're going to have some fun." Bypassing the people at the door, I walked right up to the bouncer with the shaved head, grinning wide; his name was Zane, an up and coming UFC champ. Holding out my hand, he shook it and slapped me on the shoulder.

"It's good to see you, Avery. I didn't know you were in town until Andrews told me what he did to your girlfriend." Aylee rolled her eyes and he laughed. "He and Megan are both inside. He's getting ready for a fight."

"You're not fighting tonight?" I asked him.

"Nope, that's tomorrow at the MGM Grand. You should both come. It'll be one hell of a battle."

Glancing over at Aylee, she shrugged. "I don't see why not. That's if we aren't chasing down the bad guys."

Zane chuckled. "I would've given my left nut to see you take down Andrews. The guys at the gym are still talking about it."

"I should've been kicking this one's ass," she said, elbowing me in the side. "He's the one who doubted me."

Zane turned his sly gaze to mine. "I'm pretty sure he's learned his lesson by now."

I snorted. "You have no idea."

Stepping out of the way, he waved his hand toward the door. "Have fun. I'll see you in there later."

We headed straight for the bar and ordered drinks. Once she had her screwdriver and I had my gin and tonic, I led her to the main attraction. In the ring, there were two fighters pummeling each other, one covered in blood while the other dominated. "Have you ever tried getting in the ring?" she asked.

"I've thought about it, why?"

Shrugging, she brought her drink to her lips, her

eyes twinkling. "Just asking. I think you'd look pretty sexy up there kicking some guy's ass."

"Maybe one day I'll show you. Tonight, however, I want us to have some fun. And then when we get back to hotel, we'll have an even better time."

She bit her lip. "Or maybe I won't be able to wait until we get home. An awful lot can happen in a long car ride . . ."

I groaned just thinking about it. She knew how to get me primed.

"If it isn't Little Red Riding Hood and the big bad wolf," Kyle teased, walking up from behind.

Shaking my head, I turned around and laughed. "I'm the hunter, not the wolf, Andrews."

Kyle stood there with his fists wrapped, with Megan by his side. She pointed at him and whispered loudly so we all could hear. "Don't let him fool you, he's the big bad wolf."

Picking her up around the waist, he kissed her and wouldn't let her go. "Better watch out or I might eat you."

"Don't threaten me with a good time," she laughed making Aylee snicker. When Kyle sat her down, she held her hand out to Aylee. "I'm Megan. I heard about what this bonehead did to you. You're Aylee, right?"

Aylee shook her hand and nodded. "It was this one who instigated it," she said, pinching my arm.

Megan winked at me. "They like to underestimate us, but you showed them. I hate that I missed it."

"All right, I'd love to stay and bullshit with you, but my fight's about to start. Drinks after?" Kyle asked.

I shook his hand. "Sounds like a plan."

We all three took seats and Aylee held onto my hand, smiling wide as she glanced around the room. "I like it here. The energy is amazing. We don't have things like this where I'm from."

"We do in Charlotte. Maybe one day you can check it out."

All she did was smile and give me a nod.

My statement had been made to gauge her reaction to Charlotte, but she didn't give me much to go on. There were so many things I wanted to say to her, but the last thing I wanted to do was freak her out. I needed to talk to her about what we were going to do when the case was over, but everything that came to mind made me sound like a selfish fool. I didn't want to let her go, but I couldn't ask her to give up her life in Maine either. The question was . . . what would I be willing to give up to join her?

CHAPTER 28

AYLEE

I had no clue what to say to Jason's remark. I would love to visit Charlotte, but for what, a weekend? That would be the only time we'd see each other. Two days here, two days there. Would that really work? I didn't know what to say so I smiled and nodded my head. By the look in his eyes, I could tell it wasn't exactly what he wanted. But what did he want me to say?

Kyle's fight was amazing and I enjoyed every minute of it. After he kicked his opponent's ass, he joined us at the bar for a couple of drinks. While Jason and Kyle were immersed in a conversation, Megan slid her stool closer to mine. "How do you like Vegas?"

I shrugged. "It's okay. I'd probably like it more if it

wasn't for work. Having to deal with the people we're investigating really makes me lose faith in humanity."

"Trust me, I know. I've dealt with my fair share of pain. You and Jason seem to click really well with each other. How long have you two been working together?"

"About six weeks."

She choked on her drink. "Really? Wow, I thought you two knew each other longer than that."

I shook my head and finished the last of my screwdriver. "I'm from Maine. Jason actually hated me when I showed up at his doorstep."

She nudged me in the side. "Don't worry, that's how Kyle and I were at the beginning. I despised him. And now look at us, we're engaged. Are you two serious now?"

"For the moment." We continued talking and I realized we really meshed well. I couldn't say that about many women. All my life I had only guy friends. It was nice having a female my age to talk to. Not wanting to have this conversation with Jason beside me, I nodded toward the dance floor. "Want to dance?"

Placing her hand over heart, she stood. "I thought you'd never ask."

I slapped Jason on the shoulder. "Going to dance. Don't be jealous." Before he could say anything, I took off with Megan and smiled over my shoulder at him. He and Kyle both turned around in their stools so they could watch us.

"I think we got their attention," she shouted. Jason watched me with his heated gaze and I shivered. Megan moved closer and grabbed my hands. "I think he just answered my question."

"What do you mean?"

She looked over at the guys and then back to me. "That boy is in love with you. It's written all over his face."

"I know he loves me, that's not the problem."

"What is then?"

"We live too far apart."

She rolled her eyes and twirled me around. "So? You can always relocate."

"True, but he hasn't even mentioned it. I don't even know if that's what he wants."

"And you're afraid you'll look needy if you bring it up first?" I nodded, realizing it for the first time. She twirled me around again and pulled me close, her voice right by my ear. "Things will all work out. I'm a firm believer of that. Before you leave Vegas I have no doubt this conversation will come up. All you'll have to do then is make a decision."

"What if we don't talk about it before we go our separate ways?"

"Then if it's meant to be you'll find your way back to each other."

"You and Megan seemed to get along well," Jason mentioned, grabbing my hand. He ended up dancing with me for a while at the club, but then we left to spend the rest of the evening by ourselves. We were at the very top of the Stratosphere, gazing out at the city of lights below us.

"We did. It was nice having a female my age to talk to. I grew up kind of being a loner so I didn't have that many girlfriends. I guess you can say I wasn't the prom queen type."

"You'd never believe it now."

"What about you? Tell me about your life at home, your friends. What kind of house do you live in?" I asked.

He chuckled. "I don't know where to begin. Where I live is actually a small city right on the outskirts of Charlotte. My house isn't much. It's just a three bedroom ranch, but I own the ten acres it's on. I know that's probably small compared to what you're used to."

"No, I think it's great. When I picture Charlotte, I think of the tall high rises and horrible traffic."

"Which is why I don't live in the big city. I like having my own space where it's quiet. My friends are what makes it home for me though." He pulled me in close. "Would you believe I'm good friends with the Carolina Cougars?"

"The football team?" I asked.

"Yep. We all hang out at this tavern in town. It's one of the best places to eat in North Carolina. After I helped one of their players on a case, I became really close to them. It's funny because all the people from home are like my family."

"Sounds amazing."

"It is. Now, where my best friend is concerned, you'd either love him or hate him. Luke's a motocross racer and a complete jackass at times, but he's never let me down. When my sister died, he was right there for me. It was hard when my parents blamed me for her death."

"I can imagine. Sometimes I blame myself for my parents' deaths. If I'd only ran faster for help or tried to find something for a weapon."

Jason gripped my shoulders, turning me to face him. "You'd be dead right now. You were only eight years old."

"I know. I just wish I would've tried harder." A tear slid down my cheek.

"You can't beat yourself up over that, Aylee. I have scars all over my back from the fire, but I know I tried my hardest to save my sisters. That's all that matters. The same goes for you. It might've taken you a few years, but you got your revenge. The fuckers who killed your mother are dead."

More tears fell and he wiped them away. "I know something's bothering you. What is it?"

I shrugged. "Lots of things I guess. Once this is over, you have so much to go back to. I'm envious. I have my uncle and the B&B. And now my best friend moved to New York."

He brushed the curly tendrils away from my face. "I thought you were a loner."

"I don't want to be anymore."

Holding my face in his hands, he lowered his lips to mine. I held him tight and didn't want to let go. "It doesn't have to be like that, firecracker." He kissed my temple and spoke into my hair. "Let's get back to the hotel and we can talk about it. Then afterward, I'm going to make love to you, all night long. I hope you're ready."

"I'm more than ready."

Hand in hand, we walked toward the elevators and I took one last look at the glowing city below. It was strange how something so beautiful could be filled with corruption, violence, and death. I was ready for the waiting game to be over and I knew the end was coming. Once off the elevators, we walked out to his car and drove the four miles back to the Bellagio. Instead of the valet parking, he drove us to the parking garage –

which was almost full – and parked the car himself.

"Is there a reason you don't like using valet?" I asked curiously.

We got out and started toward the elevator. "I don't know. I guess I don't feel the need when I know I'm capable of parking myself."

I held onto his arm. "Good answer. I admire that you're not like some of the people here. I'd be parking the car myself too."

He kissed the top of my head. "And that's why this is going to work."

When we got to the elevator, I instinctively reached for my gun and realized I'd left my purse in the car. "I need my purse. Hold the elevator, I'll be right back."

Putting his foot in the door, he pulled out the key fob and pressed the unlock button. I watched the lights flash and hurried over to open the door. Before I could get there, the hairs on the back of my neck stood on end. Something was wrong and it was close by. I'd been dealing with evil for a long time and I could always tell when it was near. I turned around to find a man dressed in black with a hat hung low over his eyes, sneaking up behind Jason with a two by four in his hands.

"Jason, look out!" I screamed. I tried to get the words out but my voice felt like it was moving in slow motion while the rest of the world moved on fast play. Jason didn't even have time to react before he was hit in the head with damaging force, his body dropping hard to the ground. I could see his blood on the two by four and rage consumed me. I wanted to run to him to see if he was okay, but the attacker started toward me.

My hands shook with fury and I sprang into action. Ripping open the car door, I reached for my purse but a searing pain exploded in my head. My vision blurred. What the hell? Then it hit me when another blow knocked me to my knees. There were two people.

Before the last blow dragged me into darkness, I looked over at Jason. He lifted his head and I heard his voice scream out my name before I fell into nothingness. He was alive . . . that was all that mattered.

Pain and darkness.

Whatever I was lying on was uncomfortable and felt like a ton of bricks. I tried to open my eyes and realized I was blindfolded. My hands and feet were secured by what felt like cable ties biting into my skin. The room spun and bounced as if there was an earthquake, but by the sounds and smells around me I was in a vehicle, most likely a van of sorts. There were people talking but their words were jumbled together and I couldn't make sense of their conversation.

All I knew was, I didn't have my gun and I had no

clue where they were taking me or who the hell they were. The car bounced forward and my head hit the floor, the pain causing me to hiss. But that wasn't the only thing I felt. There was a body beside me. Was it Jason? My captors grew silent and it wasn't long before I felt the presence of a person hovering above me.

"I see someone's awake," the voice said low.

I froze and tried to concentrate on the voice. Everything was so loud and my head throbbed to the point of agony. Fingers grazed along my cheek and then I felt a needle pierce the side of my neck. Whatever was inside burned through my veins and made everything feel heavy. I couldn't move and the voice whispering in my ear grew farther by the second.

"We have a long drive ahead of us. When you wake up, that's when the fun'll begin."

Before the medicine could knock me out, I breathed in and gasped. I knew who it was, I recognized her by the smell of her perfume.

CHAPTER 29

JASON

Machines beeped and the smell of alcohol made my nose burn. I thought I'd wake up to a fucking nightmare, but instead Ryan Griffin sat across a hospital room with a glum look on his face. I jerked up and the machines went on alert. Ryan rushed over and pushed me back down on the bed, but I grabbed his shirt, pulling him to me.

"Calm down, you idiot or they'll pump you full of sedatives."

"Where's Aylee?"

Huffing, he jerked his shirt away from me and backed up. "We don't know. The car she was taken in was found in a parking lot just down the road. It was one of Drake's."

"Does she have her gun?"

"No, it was found in your car."

"Fuck!" I tried to run my hands through my hair, but couldn't because there was a bandage and a zing of excruciating pain when I touched the back of my head. "How long have I been out?"

He cleared his throat. "A little over a day."

I felt like I'd been sucker punched in the gut. "A day? Do you have any fucking idea what she could be going through right now?"

Ryan sighed. "You have a concussion and we thought maybe a skull fracture but the x-ray came back fine. Thankfully, you have a hard head. I have everyone on my team trying to find her."

My body shook with rage and the machines started to go on alert as I ripped the IV out of my arm. "Have you looked at the video cameras in the garage? There were two people. One attacked me and the other went after Aylee."

Ryan sighed and helped me off the bed. "I knew you were going to be like this. Did you get a good look at them? We couldn't see shit in the video."

Pain exploded in my head when I shook it. I brought my hands up to hold my head still. "I didn't get a good look at the person who attacked me, but I did see the one who hit Aylee. The body clearly wasn't a man's."

"Are you saying it's a woman? Who the fuck could it be?"

"I don't know, but we're about to find out." My clothes were in a bag on the counter. Pulling them out, my shirt was covered in blood. Before I could put it on, the door burst open and a couple of nurses charged in.

"Mr. Avery, what are you doing?" one asked. She was a stout woman with short brown hair and a masculine build.

Baring my ass to the room, I ripped off the hospital gown and put on my jeans. "I'm getting out of here."

"You have a concussion and we need to run more tests to make sure you're all right. If I have to call security I will."

I threw the bag in the trash and stalked toward her. The other nurse backed up but she stood firm. "You can call security, but nothing's going to stop me. I'm the only one who can find my partner and I'll be damned if I let you or anyone else stand in my way. You can run whatever fucking tests you want when she's safe."

Ryan pulled out his badge, showing it to her. "I'm Ryan Griffin, Chief of Police. You can let him go."

The woman stepped aside and I rushed past, followed by Ryan. My whole body ached but I didn't give a damn. I'd run a fucking marathon if I knew it would get Aylee back home and safe. "Where's my phone?"

"It was smashed on the ground when we found you."

"Goddammit," I shouted, punching the elevator button. "Take me to the hotel. I can use my laptop. What about my gun?"

"It's in my car."

"Good, I'm going to need it."

Pulling up to the front of the hotel, the valet attendants gave us a wide berth; especially me considering my shirt was covered in blood. I ran through the lobby straight to the elevators with Ryan on my heels.

"What if I'm too late?" I rushed into the elevator, pacing like a caged animal. "Fuck, how could I be so goddamned stupid?"

"We'll find her. Just do what you have to do and we'll be on our way."

"I sure hope you're right." The elevator doors opened and I ran to our room. Once inside, I booted up my laptop and rushed to find a change of clothes. My hair was matted with dried up blood but I didn't care. Ryan grabbed a bottle of water from the refrigerator and set it beside my laptop.

"Drink something. I can't have you dying on me before we get there."

I sat down and my fingers went ninety miles an hour as I typed in the codes. It was something I'd learned a long time ago.

"What are you doing?"

"When Aylee was brought into this mission, I put trackers on her personal items. It was the only thing I knew that would work." I continued to type away and was almost there.

Ryan slapped me on the shoulder, figuring it out. "Well, I'll be damned. Does she know?"

I shook my head, remembering that night all too well. "We argued one night and I left. I didn't really leave, I just went downstairs and blew some money away. After my head cleared, I snuck into her room and inserted trackers into her things. The main one being her gun but that doesn't help, considering she doesn't have it. Now all I have to do is pray that she's wearing one."

Taking a deep breath, I typed in the last button and waited on the results to calculate. One by one, the trackers started to show up on the screen. Most of them were in the hotel with one out in the parking deck that was most likely her gun still in my car.

"Is that all of them?"

"No . . ." I zoomed out and found a blinking light. "There she is," I said, zooming back in so I could pinpoint the address. It was three fucking hours away. "Jesus. We need a helicopter, now. Can you get one?" Slamming the laptop down, I put it under my arms and stormed toward the door.

"Where is she? I'll call it in."

Rushing down the hall, I felt everything crushing in all around me. If anything happened to her I was going to make sure someone paid for it. The elevator door opened and I marched inside, my body coiled and ready to fight. "Arizona. Now get me the fuck there."

CHAPTER 30

AYLEE

I drifted in and out of consciousness, not knowing for how long or what day it was. My head still hurt but I was actually on a soft bed this time and not just thrown on the floor. What I really wanted to know was if it had been Jason beside me in the car. And if it was, was he okay?

My arms felt heavy but my wrists weren't tied like they were in the vehicle. Air conditioning blew across my bare skin, making me well aware that I was only in my bra and underwear. I was afraid to open my eyes for fear of what I'd see. When I opened them, I was met with darkness. Only a small amount of light was filtering into the room through a crack in the door. There were no windows; no possible route of escape.

Voices could be heard in the next room and I immediately recognized the high pitched whine of Georgia Blackwell. I remembered her voice in my ear and the smell of her perfume. As soon as I got the chance, I was going to put a bullet through her fucking brain. The other voice, however, sounded vaguely familiar, but it definitely wasn't Drake.

The bed creaked as I moved across it, my feet touching the cold and smooth floor. My stomach rolled with the smell of death permeating the air. Not many people could pinpoint the odor, but after witnessing horrific murder scenes it was a smell you couldn't forget.

Georgia was speaking. "What the hell are we waiting for? Let's finish this and get out of here. The sooner they find them, the sooner this can be over and we can be together."

I moved closer, hoping to hear the other person's voice. The only reply from him was a grunt. I finally got to the door and peeked through the crack. I could see her with her arms crossed, a disgruntled look on her face, leaning against a long wooden table in her black lingerie.

Considering there were no windows, we had to be in a basement. However, that wasn't my biggest concerned. For when she moved away from the table, I got a good view of the ropes and chains on both ends, stained red. The source of the stale blood smell. It wafted to my nose and I threw a hand over my mouth to stop from gagging. I breathed through my mouth, trying desperately to think up an escape plan. There were two of them and only one of me. I couldn't even see the stairs leading to the upper levels. *Fuck, fuck, fuck.*

Georgia stormed over to a corner, but I couldn't see that far. "Are you even listening? Turn around and talk to me, dammit!" The next thing I heard was a slap and the sound of her choking. With a hand around her throat, she was hauled back to the table and I hid out of sight, putting my back against the wall.

"Why don't you shut the fuck up for once," he growled. Clothes ripped and she yelped, but it wasn't in pain.

"Oh my God, yes," she moaned.

The sound of bodies smacking together made me sick. What the hell just happened? I peered around the side and that was when I got a good look at the man who was fucking her from behind, jeans halfway down his legs. *No fucking way.* I may have only seen the guy once, but he was the spitting image of his father.

Drake's son. God, what was his name . . . Blaine? Eww, she was fucking her stepson. *You have got to be kidding me.* In complete and utter shock, I couldn't take my eyes away from the disgusting display. It didn't take a genius to figure out what the whole scheme was about. Drake was probably the clueless bastard in the whole thing.

Blaine was done getting his jollies in just a few seconds, but he held her down on the table with a hand at her neck. She tried to lift up, but he forced her back down. "When are you going to stop wearing condoms? I want to feel you come inside me."

His other fist clenched. "You mean like my father does? Did he come inside you when you fucked him last night?" I could hear the anger in his voice and I held back a gasp. The whole situation was too fucked up to even wrap my head around.

"Blaine, that's not . . . I didn't . . ."

He pulled out of her and before I could even attempt to help, he swiftly grabbed the knife on the table and slid it across her throat. I slapped a hand over my mouth and closed my eyes, trying hard to keep from making a sound. It had to be a bad dream. Surely, I didn't just see that happen? Unfortunately, I could hear Georgia choking on her own blood and then the sound of her body as it crashed to the floor.

Think, Aylee. I had to get out of there, but how? Opening my eyes, I took a deep breath and peered through the crack again. Blaine ripped off the condom and wrapped it in a paper towel before shoving it in his jeans pocket. The bloody knife was on the table but still within his reach. If I raced out now, he could easily grasp it and attack.

"I know you're watching," he called out. Eyes wide, I stepped back, my pulse racing. His eyes transfixed on mine through the crack and he smiled. "Did you like the show?" Strolling to the door, he pushed it open and leaned against the frame, all cool and casual as if he didn't just kill someone. His hands were covered in blood and he had droplets on his chest and face. The metallic smell of it made me nauseated. "Can't speak?" he asked, eyes gleaming.

"No."

His eyebrows lifted in amusement. "No, you can't speak? Or no, you didn't like the show?"

"No, I didn't like the show. Happy?" I huffed.

The wolfish smile on his face spread wider as he stepped forward. "Much," he said, wiping his bloody hands on his jeans. "I couldn't wait to get rid of that cunt. She never knew when to keep her mouth shut."

"So it was her who hit me over the head and you with Jason? Where is he?"

His eyes raked over my body. "He's fine, probably in the hospital. I can't say the same for you though. You woke up a lot earlier than expected."

"Trust me, I'd have preferred not seeing you fuck your stepmother and then slice her throat open."

His eyes widened. "No wonder my father couldn't wait to fuck you again."

"I didn't fuck your father," I hissed.

"No? He said he did. Why would he lie?"

"Because I made him think we did. I can be quite persuasive."

He stared at me. "Intriguing. You're not reacting the way I thought you would. Most women would be scared right now, especially after watching me kill someone. One would almost think you've seen it before."

I had seen death and it scared me, but I wasn't afraid of him. I was afraid of not having a plan. "I have killed people, Mr. Blackwell. So maybe it's *you* who should be afraid of *me*."

Holding the door open, he waved me forward, holding back his chuckle. "Whatever you say. Let's go."

"Where are we going?"

"Upstairs. Not unless you want to stay down here with a rotting corpse." When I didn't move, he pursed his lips, losing patience. "Either you move those feet of yours or I'll drag you upstairs by your hair. Personally, I'd rather not because I kind of like that red hair of yours, besides I'm sure you have a screaming headache right now."

It was true, I did. Taking a deep breath, I let it out slowly and took my first step. I kept my head held high and walked past him, only for him to grab my arm.

"Good girl. It's time to get you cleaned up."

"Cleaned up for what?"

"You'll see. But I think right now we could both use a shower." He winked down at me and my stomach clenched.

Gripping my arm tight, he walked me past Georgia's corpse and the torture table, managing to get us by without stepping on the blood. I could only imagine the kind of torment the other women had endured while being stuck down there. He flipped off the lights like it was no big deal to leave a dead body on the floor. There was a long hallway with multiple doors. The one he chose led up a set of stairs to another shut door.

I willingly followed him up, knowing very damn well anything was going to be better than the basement. When he opened the door, I squinted my eyes away from the sunlight. My heart sank. It was daylight, which meant I'd been gone for hours, if not days. "Who's house is this?"

He jerked me across the marble floors. "My father's. He never came up here."

"Let me guess, it's where you and Georgia came to kill the other women? This house reeks of death."

Stopping mid-step, he turned to face me, eyes narrowed. "What do you know about that? There hasn't been anything in the media."

Pushing me into one of the bedrooms, I tripped over the carpet and fell. I looked around the room for anything I could use as a weapon and smiled. I had lots of choices. "Yes, I know. Your daddy made perfectly sure it wouldn't be. However, secrets only stay hidden for so long. Tell me, does he have any idea about your extracurricular activities?"

"No, but he will soon. Now get undressed and get in the shower. We need to clean up."

"We?"

He scoffed. "Surely you didn't think I was going to leave you out of my sight." Undoing his jeans, he let them fall to the floor. I made no move to get out of my bra and underwear. "We can do this the easy or the hard way. Your choice."

I was a good distance away from him and if I could just get to the door, I might have a chance at escape. He stepped forward and I stepped back toward the dresser, reaching behind my back like I was unlatching my bra. All I had to do was grab the lamp. As fast as I could, I twirled and snatched it, swinging it around with my body, smacking him across the head. The thing shattered and I took off.

"Son of a bitch," he growled, grabbing his head.

I didn't waste time racing out the door. The house was huge and I had no idea where to go. If I had to dive out of a window I'd do it. He wasn't behind me and I breathed a sigh of relief as my salvation seemed within reach. I was so close to the front door. Then Blaine flew out of nowhere and tackled me to the floor.

"Looks like you want it the hard way." His fist lifted high in the air and it was the last thing I saw before it connected to the side of my cheek. I saw stars as pain exploded in my head, but then the darkness took over. I had failed.

CHAPTER 31

AYLEE

My jaw throbbed and I groaned as I tried to lift my head, the silky sheets below me sticking to my face with dried blood.

"You are going to be one brain dead bitch by the time I get through with you," Blaine griped. He grabbed my bound wrists and roughly hoisted me to stand on my shackled feet. The room spun and I almost fell, but he lifted me in his arms.

I didn't even have the strength to fight. "You're not going to get away with this." Laughing, he kicked the bathroom door open and dropped me to the floor. I couldn't break the fall since my hands were tied and ended up landing on my hip. "So help me God, if you put another bruise on my body I'm going to rip your dick off."

He turned on the shower and the steam started to fill up the room. "Not if it's inside your pussy," he taunted, lifting me up by the arm. I could only take tiny steps with my bound ankles. Once I got to the shower, he pushed me the rest of the way in, my shoulder slamming into the tile wall. "Do you think anyone's going to care what happens to a worthless whore? Look how easily the other ones were tossed to the side."

That might've been true in the way our world was fucked up, but my people were going to make sure I was found. Jason would find me. I had to believe he would. With his hand on my neck, he forced my head under the water and it turned pink with my blood. "I'm perfectly capable of taking a shower by myself," I growled.

His body brushed up against my backside and I clenched my thighs together as hard as I could. Thoughts of him raping me ran through my mind. I wasn't going down without a fight.

"I know you can, but I thought it'd be more enjoyable this way." He washed my hair and more blood ran down the drain. Adrenaline surged through my veins so hard, I didn't even notice the pain. I concentrated on keeping my body alert and my legs tight. Taking the bar of soap, he reached around my waist and rubbed it over my stomach. I tensed and hissed when he lifted it to my breasts. "Just relax," he murmured in my ear.

"Fuck you."

Slamming me against the wall, he forced his cock between my legs, sliding it against my thighs. "I bet you want me to fuck you right now. If I was to jam my dick inside you I'm sure it'd slide right in, wouldn't it?" My breaths came out in rapid pants as I prepared myself to fight. Luckily, it didn't come to that. He pulled back – letting my neck go – and washed himself off, chuckling under his breath. "Before I fuck you, we're going to have some fun first." Shutting off the water, he jerked me out and I stood there as he dried off his body and then mine, smiling at my torment. "I think it's time we say hello to our guest of honor."

Lifting me in his arms, I felt exposed and completely vulnerable not wearing any clothes as he carried me through the house. I had a feeling I knew who the guest of honor was going to be. Once up the stairs, he carried me into another bedroom, but this one was larger, almost exactly like the same room I had been in back in Vegas.

Drake was on the bed, pale and struggling to breathe. When his eyes caught mine, they widened. "What's going on?"

Blaine dropped me into one of the chairs and marched over to a dresser. He pulled out a set of lingerie and a pair of clean jeans from a duffle bag hidden in the corner, along with a large knife. "You're about to die. That's what's going on," he announced.

Drake furrowed his brows, clearly delusional. "I don't understand."

Rolling his eyes, Blaine came over to me and slid the knife through the cable ties, freeing me. "Fucking idiot," he mumbled under his breath. Then to me he said, "If you so much as try to escape again, I will gut you nice and slow, so you feel every fucking rip of your muscles." He tossed the black, lacy babydoll lingerie onto my lap. "Put that on."

Not wasting any time, I slid it on, thankful I wasn't naked anymore. "What did you do to him?"

Blaine walked over to his father. "He took a few too many pain pills this morning."

"No," Drake choked out. "I did no such thing."

Blaine lifted Drake's chin with the knife. "Yes, you did. You've been distraught over murdering those whores you've been sticking your dick in and now you went over the edge after murdering your wife. You couldn't handle the guilt."

"This makes no sense. Wh—why are you . . . what is going on? Where's Georgia?"

Watching Blaine torment his father made me sick to my stomach. I never noticed it the night I met him, but he looked at Drake with utter disdain. What could've ever made a son turn on his own father like that? Blaine licked his lips and sneered. "She's dead. After I fucked her in the ass, I slit her throat. You should thank me. It was her idea to blackmail you in the first place."

"*She* wanted to kill the girls?" I gasped.

Drake was clearly out of it and not understanding a word that was being said. Blaine slid the knife away from Drake's chin – cutting it – before focusing on me. "She was jealous when she found out my father was cheating on her with common whores. That's when I came into the picture and started fucking her. Together we came up with a plan to get him out of our lives for good.

She was one evil bitch when it came to those cunts. After I was done with them, she liked to fuck them up. And as you're aware, nobody cares if someone like you shows up dead. We tried to pin the murders on my father, but money and power in this city buys silence. That's why I had to step it up a notch."

"I bet Georgia didn't know she was going to see the edge of your knife on this deal," I countered.

He scoffed. "She was falling apart. When I caught her fucking him last night," he said, pointing the knife at Drake, "I knew she had to go."

"What was all of this for? Why would you kill your own family, not to mention countless other women?"

His lips spread into an evil grin. "Money, power. I'll finally have it *all* once I take over his part of Randall

Enterprises. I'll be untouchable."

I shook my head, appalled. "Untouchable, my ass. You're nothing but a spoiled, greedy bastard. This plan isn't just going to blow up in your face, it's going to fuck you in the ass."

"You are so clueless, it's sad. Let me guess, you flunked hair school. Is that why you became a whore?"

I wasn't about to tell him who I was, but even if I didn't escape, he'd left around so much evidence that he was involved. His DNA was everywhere. *Talk about being fucking clueless.* Instead, I lied. "Actually, it was dental school, asshole."

Blaine laughed. "You sure do have a smart ass mouth. I'm surprised you haven't already been beaten to death."

Clenching my teeth, I kept my wits about me and waited patiently for the right time to strike. Something had to give. I had no energy, but I sure as hell had the determination. Drake started convulsing on the bed and I shot up out of the chair. "Oh my God!"

Blaine circled around and rushed over to him. With his attention temporarily distracted, I sprang into action. I didn't go for the door like a normal person; instead, I charged toward him. Wrapping my arms around his waist, I tackled him into the wall, slamming his head against it. The knife fell from his grasp and he growled in anger. I hit him in the nose with my knee, his blood splattering all over me. As hard as I could, I struck my elbow down on his kidney, and his knees hit the floor. I tried to jump around him, but he grabbed my legs and I toppled like a ton of bricks.

"You stupid, goddamn cunt," he spat. He tried to pull me toward him, but I held onto the bed post and reached for the knife.

It was so close.

Letting out a guttural scream, I kicked him over and over until his grip loosened just a bit. It gave me the leverage I needed to move that last inch. With the knife in hand, I swung it back and sliced him across the chest. Blood poured from the wound and his eyes grew dark.

"You're gonna wish you were fucking dead by the time I get through with you." He slapped me so hard across the cheek, I saw stars and dropped the knife. It went skittering across the floor, but now I had his weight on me. His hands were everywhere, his blood smearing across my skin as he pushed his body into mine.

"Get off of me," I screamed, trying desperately to push him away. I jammed my finger into the gash on his chest and he roared in pain. Elbowing him in the face, I slid out from under him and scrambled to get to my feet. Before I could even get my footing, his body tackled into mine and we came down hard. I cried out in pain, knowing my body was close to shutting down.

Pulling my arms behind my back, he roughly pushed

me into the floor, his hot breath on my ear. "I thought I was going to have a little fun with you, but it looks like I'll be fucking your dead corpse instead."

"Good luck trying to pin it on your father," I hissed.

He pushed his arousal into my backside. "Don't worry, sweetheart. As soon as I'm done, I have plenty of my father's spooge to put inside you, thanks to his many fucks."

"You've seriously lost your goddamned mind." In that moment, I knew my time had come to an end. I envisioned the last time I saw Jason smile and held that memory in my mind. If I was going to die I wanted him there with me, even if he was just in my heart. But there was one thing for certain, I would go down fighting. "I don't give a rat's ass what you do to me," I hissed. "I'm happy knowing that once Jason finds you he'll rip you into fucking pieces."

He gripped a handful of my hair, jerking my head back. "And how is he going to find out?"

"Because I'm an FBI agent cocksucker. Enjoy being ass raped when you go to prison. You're going to have the whole bureau coming down on your head."

He froze and I could just imagine the look on his face, but I used that moment of shock to act. As hard as I could, I reared my head back and hit him in the nose, the sound of it cracking making me cringe. I rolled to the side and away from him. Blood poured from his nose and his eyes were on fire as he got to his feet, stalking toward me.

I kept rolling away until a voice screamed my name from below. I gasped, thinking I had to have imagined it, but Blaine reacted to it as well. He was there. Jason was actually there.

"Aylee!"

"Jason!" I screamed back, desperate for him to hear me. "Jason, hurry!" His footsteps thundered up the stairs and he wasn't alone. Blaine grabbed the knife off of the floor and charged toward me. "Jason, *please*!"

The door burst open just as Blaine ripped me off the floor and put the knife to my throat. Tears streamed down my cheeks when I finally got to see Jason, his gun drawn and pointing right at Blaine's head. The second he got a good look at me, his eyes blazed.

"You found me," I whispered, the knife cutting my skin as I spoke.

"I'll always find you," he promised, turning his murderous glare to Blaine. "Let her go," he commanded.

Blaine chuckled and gripped me tighter. "Drop your gun and I will."

What I thought would end up being a stand-off turned out to be the opposite. Without hesitation, Jason pulled the trigger and everything moved in fast forward. Blaine's hold on my hair loosened and he fell to the floor, the knife grazing across my neck. My ears rang from the shot and I stood there stunned into silence as I looked down at Blaine's still form, his head split open, gushing blood. More officers stormed into the room, and Jason picked me up in his protective arms, shielding me from view.

Ryan draped a blanket over me and Jason rushed me out of the room, the chief hot on his heels. "Blackwell's still alive, but barely. An ambulance should be here soon."

"Oh my God, Georgia," I called out. Jason stopped and they both looked at me. "She's dead. Blaine killed her. She was a part of this whole thing."

Ryan's mouth gaped open. "You can't be serious?"

"She's in the basement." Ryan nodded and took off toward the basement, commanding some of the other officers to join him. "Please get me out of here," I begged, clutching Jason's shirt. He rushed me outside and the driveway was packed with police cars. The ambulances pulled in and he carried me toward them.

"You're okay," he whispered, holding me tight. "Thank fucking God you're going to be okay."

"Don't let me go," I cried. "Whatever you do, don't ever let me go."

"I don't plan on it."

I woke up to bright lights and the sound of beeping machines. Jason held my hand, but his head was down, breathing slow and deep. I didn't want to wake him so I laid back and watched him. "I'm alive because of you," I whispered, not thinking he could hear me.

He squeezed my hand and his head lifted, green eyes weary. "I was almost too late."

A tear fell down my cheek. "But you weren't. Did I pass out in the ambulance?"

He nodded. "You've been out for a few hours. You were dehydrated with a lump on your head the size of mine. Luckily, the two by four didn't break my skull. I guess we both have hard heads." Pausing, he released a heavy sigh, his body tense. "They ran some other tests as well to see if you were . . . violated."

"I wasn't," I claimed truthfully. I was pretty sure I'd have known if I was. "I thought he was going to, but I wasn't going to go down without a fight."

"I know, but it scared the fuck out of me when they told me they were going to check for it. I didn't want to imagine you going through that. From the looks of you, I just knew that fucker had raped you. His death should've been painful, but I couldn't gamble with your life."

A tear rolled down my cheek. "I thought I was never going to see you again."

"So did he," Ryan said, entering the room with a

sad smile. "He was a crazed man once he awoke in the hospital. Couldn't blame him though. I'd have been the same way if it was my wife." Jason's jaw clenched, his gaze focused on our entwined hands.

"I'm assuming you want my story?" I asked.

Nodding, he sat down in the chair to my other side. "Is it too soon, or do you need more time?"

"No, I can do this, but first, what's the status on Drake? Is he alive?"

"For now. Don't know how he'll be when he finds out what happened. Out of all the people it could've been, I never thought it'd be his son."

"And his wife," I added. "She was the one who used the knife on the others. She was jealous of Drake sleeping with them. That's when she started messing around with Blaine, who only ever wanted his dad's position and power. Apparently, they came up with the whole blackmail scheme together. After the first murder, they thought it would be pinned on Drake, but it never happened. That's why they continued to kill, in hopes it would lead to him."

"And I bet Drake paid off the media to keep suspicion away from him. It would clearly ruin his image."

I nodded. "I guess you can't blame the guy considering he was innocent, but it still doesn't change the fact that he could buy people's silence. If he was actually the killer, he could've easily gotten away with murder."

"Why do you think I got you two involved?" Ryan countered.

"Because we're the best," I said, hoping to brighten Jason up. I winked at him and he smirked.

"Is there anything else?"

I shook my head. "I think that's it. I'm just glad it's over. My only regret is that we couldn't save any of the other girls."

Ryan stood and walked around to Jason, placing his hand on his shoulder. "You did good, son, both of you," he added, meeting my gaze. "Once everything's settled, I'm sure you'll be heading back home, correct?"

"I guess so," Jason replied. "I have some people I want to say goodbye to and I'm sure Aylee does as well." I did, but the thought of telling everyone goodbye made my chest ache.

Ryan held out his hand and Jason shook it. "Just make sure to stop by and see me before you go. I can't begin to tell you how much I appreciate everything you've both done."

"Thanks, chief. I think we're going to need a vacation after this."

"That's an understatement," I added with a laugh.

Ryan smiled at us both and backed away toward the door, leaving Jason and I alone. We stared at each other for the longest time, his fingers tracing softly up my arm and back down to my hand. Lifting my hand to his cheek, he closed his eyes. "I love you, Aylee. I was so afraid I'd never be able to say it to you ever again." When he opened his eyes, a tear slid down his cheek. It was my undoing.

"I love you too. But there's one thing I need to know."

"Anything," he murmured.

"How were you able to find me?"

Rubbing the back of his neck, a sheepish grin spread across his face. "Let's just say it all started the night I snuck into your room."

CHAPTER 32

AYLEE

One Week Later

"He hasn't said a word about you two staying together or making things work?" Diane asked incredulously.

I scooped a huge bite of her famous broccoli and cheese quiche into my mouth and rolled my eyes. "Nope, and tomorrow's our last night in Vegas."

"Why don't you ask him then? You both love each other, so why not?"

"You know why I don't."

She snorted. "You don't want to look needy. I swear, for a girl who runs head first into danger you sure do cower at the thought of love. Makes no sense."

I sighed. "I just don't want to hear him say he can't

do it, that it'd be too hard."

"Do you think it will?"

"I know it won't be easy living that far away from each other, but I'm willing to try."

"That's the first step, sweetheart. I'm sure he's thought about all of this and is just waiting for the right time. You still have until tomorrow night. Just be patient."

"The right time would've been days ago. He's already booked his flight home."

"Have you?"

I looked down at my food and sighed. "Not yet. I told him I did, but I kept hoping something would change. With him scheduling his flight it's obvious he's going home no matter what."

"Where is he? I'm surprised you aren't with him."

"He's saying goodbye to his fighter friends at the gym. We've been so busy this week at the station, we haven't had time to see everyone. But I had to make sure I saw you before I left."

Her eyes misted over and she smiled. "I appreciate that. Veronica wanted me to give you this," she said, pulling out a long, black box from her purse. "It's her way of saying thank you."

I opened it up and gasped. Inside sat a beautiful diamond and sapphire bracelet. "Wow. I can't even imagine how much this cost."

She waved her hand dismissively. "Don't worry about that. She can afford it now that her girls and boys are back to work. She even told me to tell you that if you ever needed any of the gentlemen services, you have a membership for life."

Snickering, I pulled the bracelet out and clasped it around my wrist. "That's an amazing offer. I wonder what Jason would say if I told him?"

"I'm sure he'd get pretty angry, but it might also light a fire under his ass. I'd give it a try," she mentioned, smiling slyly.

I winked. "I think I will."

"Before you go, we need to walk down to my shop. I have some things I want to give you."

"Diane, you've already given me too much. I can't possibly accept anymore."

Gaze firm, she pursed her lips. "Do you remember what I told you the last time you were attempting to be difficult?"

I burst out in laughter. "Okay, fine, I'll stop being a pain."

When we got to her shop, she strolled right over to two large boxes sitting on the counter. "I had these flown in from New York." She pulled out some clothes from inside and held them up. "I thought you could use them in Maine. These are from my winter line." There were jackets, pants, long-sleeve blouses, and even a pair of winter boots with wool inside.

"I don't know what to say," I cried.

She packed the clothes back into the boxes and sealed them up. "You can say thank you and that you'll call me every week. That should suffice as payment."

Opening my arms, I wrapped them around her and squeezed. "Thank you for everything. I'm really going to miss you. But I promise to call every week."

"Good. And then maybe sometime soon, when you're not working, we can have a girls' weekend somewhere."

I pulled back and smiled. "I'd like that."

Grabbing a pen and notepad from the desk, she handed it to me. "Write down your address so I can ship these boxes to you. I don't want you having to worry about getting it all home."

I wrote the address to the B&B and gave the notepad back to her. "Thanks. That'll help out a lot."

Knowing my time was drawing near, she hugged me again. "I'm going to miss you, Aylee."

"I'll miss you too. Okay . . . now I need to finish packing and spend what little time I have left with Jason."

She wiped away her tears and smiled. "I know. Good luck with everything and be safe on your way home."

I started for the door and waved. "I will. Talk to you soon."

"You better."

The Vegas heat hit me as soon as I opened the door. I wasn't going to miss that at all, but if I had to deal with the heat to be with Jason, I'd do it in a heartbeat. Now all I needed to find out was if he felt the same. Love could only get you so far.

Instead of going back to the hotel straight away, I spent the last couple of hours taking pictures of the strip. I'd been around for weeks and hadn't taken a single one. I didn't even have one of me and Jason. My phone going dead was my cue to call it quits. It was only about a mile walk back to the hotel and I needed the time to myself to think. The ache in my chest grew worse knowing I only had one more day to be with him. And it hurt even more that he hadn't said a word about us continuing our relationship.

When I opened the door to our room, my eyes went wide in shock. "Oh my God," I breathed. The lingering sun shone through the tall glass windows, shining on a table set up with candles and two covered dishes. Jason stood by the window with a gin and tonic in his hand, gazing out at the city. "Jason this is beautiful."

He turned his green gaze my way, his lips tilting up in a smirk. "I thought we could spend this night alone, just you and me."

Throwing my purse on the counter, I strolled into his outstretched arms. He held me tight and I breathed him in. "I think it's a great idea. Did you have fun with Tyler and Kyle?"

Kissing the top of my head, he let me go and helped me into my seat at the table. "I did. They asked about you. I told them you were doing much better."

"I wish I could've said goodbye, but I needed to see Diane." He sat down across from me and lifted the tops of our food. We both had Oscar-style filet mignon with mashed potatoes and asparagus. It smelled like heaven.

"I understand. Was she sad?"

My eyes burned. "A little, but I promised we'd talk every week. She's shipping me a ton of winter clothes up to Maine."

"That's nice of her. Did she give you that bracelet too?" he asked, his gaze focusing on the glittering diamond bracelet.

I shook my head. "Ronnie, actually. It's a thank you present." I wanted to tell him about the other thing she offered, but I didn't want to spoil the mood.

"She sent me something too," he added, holding up his wrist. He had on a brand new watch that had to cost thousands.

I cleared my throat. "She didn't happen to offer you anything else did she?"

His brows furrowed. "No, why?"

He was speaking the truth so I didn't even bother elaborating. "No reason, I was just asking." I took a few bites of my food and looked out the window. The light show was always so beautiful at night; it was the perfect backdrop for dinner.

"I thought you would've been back earlier. What all did you and Diane do today?"

"We ate lunch at her restaurant and then we went back to her shop. For the past couple of hours, I walked down the strip and took pictures. Then I realized I don't have any of us. We need to take some together before we leave." A sly smile spread across his lips. "Why do you look like that?"

He shrugged. "No reason. We can take as many pictures as you want." We finished eating and then he waltzed up to the stereo, turning on the music. It was a slow, sensual beat with no lyrics. He held his hand out and bowed his head. "Will you dance with me?"

"Of course," I agreed, taking his hand. He twirled me around and put one arm around my waist and clasped his other hand with mine. We swayed to the music, keeping our eyes only on each other. "Will you miss Vegas?"

Smiling, he bit his lip. "I'll miss playing poker. But, at least now I have enough money to buy the land I want. I love living in the city, but I've always wanted land to build a cabin. The North Carolina mountains are amazing."

"I bet they're beautiful."

As soon as the song ended, Jason fetched his phone. "Smile, firecracker." He held me close and took a couple of pictures with us together. I then held up mine so I could have my own.

"Thanks. I just wanted to have some memories to take back with me to Maine."

His hands splayed across my back and he leaned in to kiss me. "And I'm hoping to give you plenty more tonight."

My body melted against his as he held me tight, tasting me, touching me. I opened myself up to him and let him take control. I yearned to hear him say that we'd be together, but I had a feeling it wasn't going to happen. A tear slid down my cheek, but Jason didn't seem to notice.

He hoisted me in his arms and carried me to the bedroom, lying me gently on the bed. There were lit candles around the room and it only added fuel to the heartache. "I want to make love to you, Aylee," he murmured in my ear.

"Yes," I breathed, swiping the tears from my eyes. He lifted his head to stare down at me, but the tears were gone. I didn't want him to see the evidence of my pain.

The next thing I knew, I was naked on the bed with him on top, kissing me deeply. His lips trailed down my neck to my breasts where he closed his lips around me, sucking greedily. He pulled my nipple between his teeth and I arched off the bed, groaning in pleasure.

"I love hearing you scream for me," he growled, sliding his fingers inside. I gasped and rocked my hips against his hand. "Fuck, I love how wet you are." Pulling his fingers out, he stuck them in his mouth and groaned. Pressing his cock against my opening, he teased me.

I wrapped my legs around his waist and tried to take him myself, but he chuckled, circling his hips to tease me more. "Please," I begged, "I need to feel you inside me."

Smile fading, his hands came up to my face and held me in place so I had no choice but to look at him. Then, I cried out as he slammed into me in one hard thrust. He moved slowly at first, my breaths coming out in rapid pants. My whole body trembled under his touch and I wanted more. Our bodies moved together perfectly as if we were always meant to be together. It all felt right, but yet seemed so difficult.

Rocking his hips against mine, that delicious ache between my legs grew stronger and stronger. My body clenched around him so hard I could feel him pulsate inside me. "Jason," I cried out, digging my nails in his back. He picked up his pace, grunting as our bodies slapped together. Everything inside me exploded as he kept going, until I felt him release his warmth deep within.

Breathing hard, he rolled us onto our sides, still connected. We'd made love until all our energy was spent. Lying face to face, he kissed my hand, his eyes growing heavy.

"When we go our separate ways, I don't want you to forget me," I whispered.

"That's not going to be possible, firecracker."

"Will you miss me?"

His eyes closed and he smiled. "Every day."

I laid there, waiting on him to open his eyes and say more, but he didn't. It was obvious we were going our separate ways. Tears fell down my cheeks, soaking the pillow beneath me, but I didn't dare let it be known. For over an hour, I watched him fall into a deep sleep until my touch couldn't even stir him.

In that moment, I made my choice.

CHAPTER 33

JASON

I woke up feeling the best I had ever felt in my life. It was my last day in Vegas and I couldn't wait to get the hell out of there and start my new life. Turning over, I found Aylee's side of the bed cold. "Aylee?" I called. There was no answer. Knowing her, she probably went down to the bakery to get some pastries. My phone beeped and I grabbed it off the nightstand.

Tyler: Everything's all ready for tonight.

Me: Good. Be there at 7.

For the past week, I'd had a lot to think about, mainly the situation with Aylee. I should've told her how I felt earlier, but I wanted everything to be a surprise. Getting out of bed, I hurried into the bathroom and took a quick shower. When I got out, I called for her again. "Aylee, you here?"

Still no answer. I threw on a pair of jeans and a T-shirt before opening the bedroom door. Everything was quiet. Sliding my wallet in my pocket, I grabbed the room key and walked out. Once the elevator took me down, I went straight to the bakery.

"Mr. Avery," Jeanine announced. She was the lady who always helped me every time I came down to get breakfast pastries. She was a petite woman with short brown hair and beady brown eyes.

"Good morning, Jeanine."

She grabbed a box and opened it. "The usual this morning?"

"Yes, please." She packaged up my pastries and I gave her my card. "You haven't by any chance seen Aylee have you?"

Her brows furrowed. "No, sugar, I haven't. I wouldn't be able to miss that red hair of hers. Is everything okay?" She handed my card back, along with the box of pastries.

"I think so. She wasn't in the room this morning. I thought she'd be down here."

She shook her head. "Sorry, I haven't seen her."

"Thanks anyway." Pastries in hand, I started toward the elevator and rode back up to the room. Once inside, I set the box down and dialed her number. It rang and rang, but she never picked up.

Me: Where are you?

I thought she'd text or call back by the time I ate breakfast, but she didn't. What the fuck was going on? Picking up the phone, I dialed her number again. After several rings, it went straight to her voicemail. "Aylee, it's me. Where are you? Call me back. I have a lot planned for us today and I can't wait to get started."

After an hour of waiting, I couldn't do it anymore. There was only one person she was close to in Vegas. I didn't care if it was stalkerish, I had to know where she was. After almost losing her once, I didn't want to imagine anything happening to her. I dialed Diane's number and she picked up on the second ring.

"Hello, Jason."

"Good morning, Diane. Have you seen or talked to Aylee this morning?"

"No, why? I wasn't planning on seeing her until the surprise party tonight. Is everything okay?"

Running a hand through my hair, I sighed. "I don't know. She's not here and she's not answering her phone."

"Hmm, that's strange. How did things go last night?" she asked curiously.

"Great, or at least, I thought they did. What all did you two talk about yesterday?"

"Lots of things. She's worried about you not wanting

to be with her because of the distance thing. I told her to be patient with you. I figured you'd tell her how you felt last night."

"I was saving it for after the party. You know what I have planned."

"I do, but she doesn't. I wasn't about to tell her."

"Fuck me. I should've known it was a mistake to wait."

She snorted. "I swear men have the worst possible timing. Aylee is an impatient woman. Making her wait to hear how you feel probably wasn't the smartest move. Are her things still there?"

I charged toward the other bedroom and slammed open the door. "Goddammit, she's fucking gone. None of her stuff is here."

"This isn't good," she added.

"No shit. I need to find her."

"Do you need her address? She gave it to me yesterday."

Rushing to my room, I threw my suitcase onto the bed, cramming my clothes into it. When I grabbed my laptop, I knew exactly what to do. "No, I know just how to find her."

CHAPTER 34

AYLEE

One call and one text. I'd been gone for almost a full day and Jason had only called me one fucking time. I almost broke down and called him back after listening to his message, but I couldn't bring myself to do it. Not after I left him in the middle of the night. I thought it'd be easier not having to deal with the awkward goodbye. By now, he most likely realized I'd left to spare us both the heartache. It was obvious he didn't mind. Luckily, I had my uncle and Regis to keep me occupied.

"Come here, Regis Finn!" I called. I didn't realize how much I'd missed the giant blanket until the moment I pulled into the driveway and he ran over the hill to greet me with his tongue lolling out to the side. He was a tri-colored, Cavalier King Charles Cocker Spaniel. Adrian had given him to me as a Christmas present one year and ever since then he had been our dog.

"What all did Adrian say when he dropped off Regis?" I asked.

My uncle put his arm around me and kissed my head. "He thought you'd want the little rascal back. From what I hear, he loves New York. Have you talked to him?"

Closing my eyes, I breathed in the cool, crisp air and then opened them. "No, but I'm glad he's happy."

We walked up to the top of a small hill over-looking the grounds, and took in the view. The white plantation style home had been transformed into a bed and breakfast back in the seventies when my uncle bought it. We had our own pond, walking trails, and wide open fields that you could get lost in for hours.

Regis hopped up on my legs. I sat down on the ground so he could tackle me. I giggled as he licked my face and lied down beside me.

"When you called in the middle of the night, I thought something was wrong."

I looked up at him, his expression troubled. "Nothing's wrong. I just wanted to come home."

He sat down beside me and rubbed Regis' head. "You can't lie to me, peanut. Is it that cop you were with? Did he do something to hurt you?"

Shaking my head, I looked away, trying desperately to keep the tears at bay. "He didn't hurt me, Uncle G. I just thought after everything we'd been through . . . it wouldn't just *end*. He never said he wanted to make things work between us once we moved home."

"Did you?"

I closed my eyes. "No."

"Then you can only blame yourself, sweetheart. You weren't raised to be scared of a fight. You fight for your country and for the good of man, maybe you should start learning how to fight for love." He squeezed my chin and then got to his feet.

"Gary!" Mitchell shouted, his voice echoing from the house. Mitchell was my uncle's significant other; they both ran the B&B together.

Gary turned around and I squinted against the sun so I could look up at him. "Yeah?" he called.

"Tell peanut she has a visitor!"

I stood up quickly, pulse racing. Regis jumped to attention and barked as I got to my feet. Was it Jason? Surely, it couldn't be him. "Who do you think it could be?"

Uncle G and I walked down the hill together, followed by Regis. "Don't know. It could be the news. I bet they want to interview you for the local paper. You're a hero now; all the people in town are proud of you."

I didn't want to be on the news again. Jason and I had more time in the spotlight in the past week than I'd care to have in my entire lifetime. When we got down to the house, I didn't see a news van anywhere, but I did see . . .

"Adrian," I gasped. He jumped off the front porch stairs and raced toward me. My heart didn't race the way it did when Jason was around, but it was still good to see him. He looked the same with his blond, spiked hair.

My uncle smiled and nudged me forward. "He was worried about you. I called him when I knew you were coming home."

Adrian scooped me up in his arms. "Thank God you're okay. I couldn't wait to see you." He set me down and Gary waved at us before disappearing inside the house. Regis ran in circles around him until he bent down to play with him. "I missed you too, Regis Finn McFadden."

"Thank you for bringing him here."

He ruffled Regis' ears and stood. "You're welcome. He's always been your dog more so than mine."

"That's probably because I snuggle him more than you."

"True," he chuckled.

"How's New York? Do you like the hospital?"

"It's amazing. I never thought I'd like living in a big city, but it's grown on me."

"And the people, are they friendly? I bet they aren't like those around these parts."

His hazel eyes sparkled. "Not all of them, but I've met quite a few who are. It's one of the reasons I wanted to talk to you. After watching the way you looked at your partner on the news, I don't feel so bad."

Grinning wide, I grabbed his hands. "Oh my God, are you seeing someone?"

He shook his head. "Not officially. She wants to be, but I wanted to clear things up with you first. I know I mentioned us getting back together, but then you left and I went to New York. It just all happened so fast."

"You don't need to explain. I'm so happy for you. Is she a doctor too?"

"She is, a very smart one at that. How about we go to dinner and catch up? I can tell you all about her and you can tell me about Vegas. I'd love to hear what happened."

Holding onto his arm, I walked with him to his car. "Brace yourself because it's one long, crazy ride. I might need a blood orange margarita or twelve to get through it."

He chuckled. "I have all weekend."

"You sure you're okay?" Adrian asked, helping me up the stairs. We'd eaten at my favorite restaurant in Hallowell that was positioned right on the Kennebec River. They made the best margaritas in town.

Giggling, I reached for one of the patio chairs and fell into it. "I'm fine. I think those margaritas were a little strong."

Adrian sat down in the chair beside me and laughed. "Well, you drank four of them. I don't blame you after what you've been through."

Sighing, I leaned my head against the house and looked out at the stars. They were so bright in the dark sky. It was something I missed in Vegas. With all the lights, you couldn't enjoy the true beauty of night. My head was fuzzy from the alcohol and all I could concentrate on was Jason. I wanted to know what he was doing and where he was at. Most importantly, I wanted to know if he missed me as much as I missed him.

"Are you thinking about him?"

"It's hard not to," I confessed.

"Then why did you leave him? You ran away when you should've stayed. It doesn't look like it made things easier. If anything, you made them a whole hell of a lot harder."

"Gee, thanks for the pep talk, pal." I shook my head and shrugged. "I don't know . . . I guess I didn't want to get hurt. At least this way, I didn't have to pretend to be strong when he turned me down. I didn't have to look in his eyes when he said it."

"Who says he was going to turn you down? You never gave him a chance."

I scoffed. "He had plenty of chances. He had the whole week."

"Maybe," he said. "I guess you'll never know."

"I guess not," I whispered. The night air grew colder and I shivered. "You about ready to head inside? I can get us some wine." I tried to get up but needed a little assistance. I wasn't drunk, but with the jet lag and time difference, it was all wearing on me.

"I think you've had enough. How about I help you to your room?"

"Sounds good. It'd suck to survive being attacked in Vegas only to come home and die from falling down the stairs."

He guffawed. "You're absolutely right. Come on." We started for the door, but a set of headlights flashed behind us. "Who would be coming in this late?"

"It's probably just some of the guests." I opened the door and took a step inside, only to be stopped by the sound of my name.

"Aylee!"

Frozen in place, I sucked in a breath, afraid to turn around. Adrian nudged me with his elbow. "Aylee, it's Jason. He came for you." Jason's footsteps grew closer until I heard him step up onto the porch. Out of the corner of my eye, I watched Adrian step forward, his hand extended. "I'm Adrian, Aylee's friend. I wanted to thank you for saving her."

Jason shook his hand, his focus completely on me. "There was no other way."

Clearing his throat, Adrian backed up toward the door. "I think I'll just go to my room and give you two some privacy." Once he stepped inside, he winked. "Good luck. See you in the morning."

As soon as he was gone, I turned to Jason, my heart thudding in my chest. His clenched jaw and tight fists spoke louder than anything. "Are you angry with me?" I asked.

He scoffed. "You mean for leaving me in the middle of the night? Yeah, just a little. What the fuck, Aylee? I woke up and you weren't there. And I guess you're back with your ex now too?"

"No! It's not what it looks like. He came here to welcome me home and to also tell me about his new love interest."

"So you didn't come back to be with him?"

Sighing, I shook my head. He was so close, I wanted

to reach out and touch him. "If you want the truth, I didn't think I could say goodbye to you. It was easier to just let you go."

He stepped forward. "Is that what you want? Because it sure as hell is not what I want."

"What? But I thought—"

"That I didn't want this to work? Have you lost your fucking mind? All you had to do was give me a little more time."

I rolled my eyes. "I gave you plenty of time."

"Not long enough. Tonight was going to be our night. I had it all planned."

"Planned? What do you mean?"

Cupping my face with his hand, I leaned into his touch, wishing he'd kiss me. "I had a whole party planned for us. Everyone was going to be there to say goodbye. Diane was helping put it together."

I gasped. "What the hell? I'm so sorry. Let me guess, she's the one who gave you my address?"

He shook his head and winked. "I have my own ways, remember?"

"Okay, *stalker*. You know that's all kinds of creepy, right? I don't know if I like being traced like that. Especially, when you can track my every move and I have no clue where you are."

His green gaze lit up in amusement. "I'm here, firecracker. And I don't plan on leaving."

"Excuse me?" I exclaimed, wide-eyed.

Chuckling, he kissed me and pressed his forehead to mine. "I lied to you the other day. I didn't purchase a plane ticket for North Carolina, I bought two flights to Maine. One for me and one for you."

"What are you saying?" I breathed.

He rubbed his thumbs across my cheeks. "I'm saying that if you want me to, I'll stay. I'll find a house and then one day when you're ready, we can take things to the next level."

"Are you flippin' serious right now?"

"More serious than I've ever been about anything. I love you, Aylee. I want this to work and I'm willing to do what it takes."

Tears streamed down my cheeks and he wiped them away. The thought was tempting, but I couldn't let him do it. "I'm sorry, Jason, but you can't leave everything for me. You have a life in North Carolina. I'm not about to take all of that away."

His hands tightened on my face, his gaze raw. "Are you saying you don't want me up here?"

I nodded. "That's exactly what I'm saying." I leaned up and kissed him gently on the lips. "Which is why I'll be going home with you." My lips spread into a wide grin as I watched him realize what I was saying.

"What about your uncle?"

"He'll be more than fine without me. Besides, it

would be selfish of me to take you away from so many people you love. I figure North Carolina could be a new adventure."

Lifting me in his arms, I could feel his heart beating against my own. "Is all of this what you were waiting for me to say?" he murmured.

I nodded. "More than anything. I just wanted to hear that nothing could stand in our way; that we could make things work."

Tucking the hair behind my ear, he smiled. "Baby, you have nothing to worry about. I don't plan on ever letting you go."

EPILOGUE

AYLEE

Six Months Later

"What do you want to do now?" I asked, climbing on top of Jason. We'd only been back three days from solving another case in Florida and I was ready to take a break. Ever since I'd moved in with him, we'd taken every single case together. Now we were on a three week vacation, free to do whatever we pleased.

Jason smiled up at me, pushing his hips into mine. "As much as I want to make love to you right now, I think we need to get something to eat."

My stomach growled. "Sounds good. The Carolina Tavern sounds mighty tasty right now."

He patted my thigh. "Then get dressed."

Rolling off of him, I jumped off the bed and went straight to the shower. North Carolina was so different from Maine. You could walk outside and be drenched in sweat in a matter of minutes. The humidity was worse than in Vegas.

I missed my uncle and the B&B, but Jason's friends had turned into my family. Diane constantly sent me presents and even came out to visit a couple of times. She loved Charlotte so much, she decided to open up a store, giving me free access to anything I would want. If I didn't take anything, she made sure to send me a package along with a letter, scolding me.

Once out of the shower, I picked out one of my many sundresses and slipped it on. The next thing I knew, Jason barreled up the steps and rushed into the room. "We have to go, now."

"Why? What's wrong?" I raced down the stairs after him.

"Something bad happened at Second Street. I got a call saying they needed backup."

I froze and looked down at my dress. "I can't go in this. Let me change really fast."

He grabbed my hand and pulled me out the door. "No time. I got your gun and badge, that's all you need."

We jumped in his car and sped out of the driveway. "Who called you?"

"One of the guys from the PD. Apparently, it's

something they can't handle."

"That makes no sense. They've handled plenty of cases without you. Besides, don't they know we're on vacation?"

He scoffed. "Like they care. Whatever it is, we'll get it handled and have the rest of the night to ourselves."

One thing I'd learned about Jason was that he was completely dedicated to the force and to solving crimes. It was one of the things I loved about him. After I moved, the bureau transferred me to another government lab based in Charlotte where I could continue to experiment. The serum turned out to be a huge success and the bureau wanted me to come up with a truth serum for interrogations. I couldn't wait to get started. When we pulled up to the Second Street Bar, there were police cars everywhere.

"Holy shit, what in the world's going on?" I exclaimed.

Jason slammed on his brakes and jumped out of the car. "I don't know, but I'm going in."

"Dammit, wait on me!" Gun in hand, I jumped out of the car and rushed inside, only to come to a freezing halt.

"Somebody might want to take her gun before she turns it on Avery," someone yelled. The crowd bellowed.

Looking around, I found Jason standing in the middle of the crowd with a mischievous smile splayed across his lips. Everyone was there, including my uncle, Diane, and even Adrian with his fiancé.

Luke, Jason's best friend, walked up to me cautiously. I had the pleasure of meeting him the day Jason brought me to Charlotte. He was definitely a ladies man with his charming smile and tousled blond hair. "Mind if I take your gun? I don't want you shooting my best friend."

I gave it to him and glanced at the people around the room before focusing on Jason.

Stepping forward, he took my hand. "Come on." He hopped up on a table and pulled me with him.

"Jason, what are you doing?"

The crowd gathered around and Diane was crying when I looked at her. What the hell was going on? Jason held up his hand and waved the crowd to silence. "Everyone, if I could have your attention. As you all know, this lovely firecracker has been here with me for six months now. I know that might not seem like a long time to some, but what we've been through surmounts any length of time. She started off as a pain in my ass—"

"Hey, look who's talking," I griped, smacking him on the arm; everyone laughed.

He pulled me close and kissed me. "Okay, so we were both pain in the asses. What I'm trying to say is, you're my partner in more ways than one. I've trusted you with my life and you've never let me down. With that being said," he murmured, getting on one knee. He reached into his pocket and pulled out a shimmering diamond ring.

Gasping, I smacked a hand over my mouth. "Oh my goodness."

Sliding the ring on my finger, he kept his green gaze on mine. "I love you, Aylee McFadden. I may drive you insane sometimes, but I hope you can see past my faults and go on this next adventure with me. Please say you'll marry me."

I pulled him up and jumped in his arms. "Yes!" I cried. The crowd cheered and I held him tight. "I love you so much."

He chuckled. "You say that now, just wait until we're eighty. You'll probably kill me by then."

"All right, you two, the fun isn't over yet," Diane called, waving her hands at us. "I have something to give you."

Jason jumped down and helped me off the table, straight into my uncle's arms. "I'm so happy for you, peanut. Promise me you'll bring the grandbabies to visit."

"Uncle G that's not happening any time soon," I laughed.

Diane ruffled my hair and whispered in my ear, "I'm sure it'll happen sooner than you expect. Hopefully, they'll take after their mother."

"I heard that," Jason grumbled.

She smiled at us both. "I have you both an engagement present. I know you're taking some time off, so it'll be perfect timing." Reaching into her bag, she pulled out a large envelope and handed it to me.

When I opened it and took a look inside, my eyes started to burn. "Diane, this is amazing. I can't believe you'd do this." Inside the envelope was an all-expense paid trip to Ireland.

"You've told me how you wanted to connect with your mother's relatives, so I thought it'd be the perfect present. You can see the land and visit your family. It's so beautiful there."

Wrapping my arms around her, I squeezed her tight and let go. "Thank you. This means a lot, really."

"You're welcome. You and Jason could use the vacation."

"That we could," he said, giving her a hug. "I thought she was going to kill me when I told her we got called in."

Diane laughed. "I can imagine. I hope you two have fun. Make sure to take lots of pictures." She winked at me and then joined her husband who was talking to a group of Carolina Cougars. Jason and his famous friends . . .

Putting his arms around my waist, he drew me into his body, placing his forehead to mine. "Are you happy?"

"Very."

"Good, because there's nothing I wouldn't give or do to make you happy."

I placed a finger on his lips. "I know, but the only thing I need is you. You're the only thing in this world that's going to make me happy. As long as you're by my side there's nothing else I'll need."

"You sure about that?"

I nodded. "It's an oath. You have my body, heart, and soul. Loving you will be the ultimate adventure."

"And loving *you* will be mine."

THE END

~Coming this August~

ROPED IN

(An **ARMED & DANGEROUS** Standalone novel)

ABOUT THE AUTHOR

NEW YORK TIMES and USA Today Bestselling author, L.P. Dover, is a southern belle residing in North Carolina along with her husband and two beautiful girls. Before she even began her literary journey she worked in Periodontics enjoying the wonderment of dental surgeries.

Not only does she love to write, but she loves to play tennis, go on mountain hikes, white water rafting, and you can't forget the passion for singing. Her two number one fans expect a concert each and every night before bedtime and those songs usually consist of Christmas carols.

Aside from being a wife and mother, L.P. Dover has written over seventeen novels including her Forever Fae series, the Second Chances series, and her standalone novel, Love, Lies, and Deception. Her favorite genre to read is romantic suspense and she also loves writing it. However, if she had to choose a setting to live in it would have to be with her faeries in the Land of the Fae.

L.P. Dover is represented by Marisa Corvisiero of Corvisiero Literary Agency.

Other Titles by
LP DOVER:

FOREVER FAE SERIES

Forever Fae

Betrayals of Spring

Summer of Frost

Reign of Ice

SECOND CHANCES SERIES

Love's Second Chance

Trusting You

Meant for Me

Fighting for Me

Intercepting Love

GLOVES OFF SERIES

A Fighter's Desire: Part One

A Fighter's Desier: Part Two

Tyler's Undoing

Ryley's Revenge

Winter Kiss: Ryley & Ashley [A Gloves Off Novella]

Paxton's Promise

Camden's Redemption

STANDALONE TITLE

Love, Lies, and Deception

ALSO CHECK OUT THESE
EXTRAORDINARY AUTHORS & BOOKS:

Alivia Anders ~ Illumine

Cambria Hebert ~ Recalled

Angela Orlowski Peart ~ Forged by Greed

Julia Crane ~ Freak of Nature

J.A. Huss ~ Tragic

Cameo Renae ~ Hidden Wings

A.J. Bennett ~ Now or Never

Tabatha Vargo ~ Playing Patience

Beth Balmanno ~ Set in Stone

Ella James ~ Selling Scarlett

Tara West ~ Visions of the Witch

Heidi McLaughlin ~ Forever Your Girl

Melissa Andrea ~ The Edge of Darkness

Komal Kant ~ Falling for Hadie

Melissa Pearl ~ Golden Blood

Alexia Purdy ~ Breathe Me

Sarah M. Ross ~ Inhale, Exhale

Brina Courtney ~ Reveal

Amber Garza ~ Falling to Pieces

Anna Cruise ~ Maverick

Also, keep reading to get a sneak peek at *Here With Me* by Heidi McLaughlin

chapter 1
Ryley

EACH STEP I TAKE IS PAINFUL. Not in the sense that I've been physically injured—unless you can count my heart being torn out and ripped to shreds, twice, as being physically hurt—but in the sense that my body aches with any type of movement. I'm sore all over from too much crying and a lack of eating. Withering away to nothing, as my best friend, Lois has been saying for the past two weeks.

The fact that it's been two weeks since my life has been turned upside down flipped inside out and run through the ringer stops me mid-step. Lois smashes into my back, no doubt looking at her phone, texting someone she shouldn't be and meddling in my affairs. Even though I love her, I want her to stop. I want to wake up from this nightmare and have my life go back to the way it was six years ago.

Lois places her hand on my back, urging me silently to take the next step, and the next one and the next one after that. She's been my rock for as long as I can remember, and surprisingly there was a time when I didn't need her as much, but that's all changed.

At the top of the staircase sits a table with a small bouquet of freshly picked flowers, a nice touch to the drab location. When Lois pulled in front of the building, I recoiled in my seat. The brick building, old and worn with age, shows no sign of being welcoming. The sidewalk is cracked and weeds grow in between the slabs. The only saving grace is the park across the street, and while it's empty, it looks inviting, if not a place to escape.

Lois opens the door before I can raise my hand to knock. She's impatient with me and I understand why. I know deep down she's afraid I'm going to turn and run. Believe me the thought has crossed my mind a time or two. I know it's not the answer, but it makes the most sense. If I can't be found, I can't be hurt, and I've had far too much hurt in my life to last me until my last breath. With her hand on my back, she gives me a gentle nudge to step into the office. The woman behind the glass wall looks up briefly and gives us a half smile. She probably feels the same way I do about the building. It's lacking in life, much like I am right now.

After giving her my name, I sit down next to Lois. Her face is now stuffed in a magazine, and she's ignoring me. This is her idea of tough love. I've been down this path with her before so I know what to expect. You'd think by now I'd be a pro and can deal with whatever is thrown my way, but I'm not. It seems that every few years my idea of happiness turns into a weak excuse for life.

My name is called, and I'm directed through an open door. The room I step into is lackluster and cold. I cross my arms to ward off an impending shiver and chastise Lois for making me wear a dress today. My cardigan is resting in the backseat of her car when it should be on my shoulders.

"Good morning. What's your name?"

It's in the chart on your desk, I want to yell out, but refrain. Lois would likely hear me and scold me like a child. I'd take it though because she'd be right. The lady behind the desk doesn't ask me to sit down or guide me to the chair or couch in her office. She doesn't even look at me. This meeting is feeling a bit too impersonal for my taste, and as I reach for the door, I hear her clear her throat.

"Ryley, I like to ask my patients to say their names so that their identities aren't forgotten when we start discussing why you're here."

It makes sense, I think. I opt to sit on the couch,

but only on the edge. I don't want to be comfortable or complacent.

"Ryley Clarke," I answer, letting my name flow easily from my lips.

"Tell me, Ryley, what brings you in today?"

Of course she wastes no time punching me in the gut. If it weren't figuratively, I'd flinch and let her know that it's not okay to hit, but instead I straighten my back and ponder the question that seems to have brought me to this point in my life. A point where I'm required, no begged, to enter therapy to help figure out the rest of my life. Maybe not even the rest, but the next step. Either step I take leads me down a path of love, pain and irreparable hurt.

Most importantly, I don't want to be here. I don't think talking to a third party with a psyche degree is the answer. Sadly, I'm the only one who feels that way. I've been told therapy will help, but I'm not so sure it will. You can't fix something that has been destroyed for years. We aren't a family of teddy bears with missing eyes or ears that can be sewn back on making us look somewhat new. We're a damaged bunch, destined for nothing but heartache.

I pick at the threadbare couch that I chose to sit on. It looked more comfortable than the chair in front of her. It's royal blue, or at least it used to be. I think at one time it was probably soft, plush and very comfortable, and people didn't have a problem lying back, closing their eyes and letting all their worries flow from their mouths. You would think that with the many people that come through the door, a new couch could be purchased. I may be wrong in my assumption. I likely am. This couch holds secrets that no one ever wants out, and it's about to know mine too. Maybe that's why she keeps it this way.

"Why am I here today?" the words are a whisper on my lips. I can barely hear them myself and know she can't hear me. Clearing my throat, I keep my eyes downcast and away from her face. The last thing I want is for her to see the pain in my eyes. That's for me and me alone when I stare in the mirror, asking myself how and why.

"I'm here so you can fix… this." The words are bitter and angry. I spread my arms out wide, and my knuckles scrape the side of the worn out armrest. I pull my right hand to me, examining my fingers for any signs of damage. A sliver maybe, something to cause pain, anything to make me feel. I have nothing.

I lean forward, determined not to cry. I don't know why I'm here. I healed. I moved on. *We* moved on. Life was good, not better, but manageable. We were happy. We laughed and loved and we missed him terribly, but we woke up each day determined to make a new happy memory. But then life — no, I take that back — the military made that all change.

If I were a conspiracy theorist, I'd say this was all planned, but honestly, what do they care about my life? Nothing, that's for damn sure. They don't care that they've ruined the last six years of my life because of some clerical error. *"Sorry,"* is all they could be bothered to say.

They're sorry.

I realize now that I've spoken, the floodgates are open, and I can't get my words out fast enough. She, the one who sits behind a desk taking notes, doesn't have a clue as to what I've been through, but I'm about to tell her.

"I don't know why I'm here. I'm not sure a session or a million sessions can fix my life right now. People have told me that time heals all wounds, but they're full of shit. I think when that saying was coined, they meant a scratch or a bump, not a hole in the middle of your chest that you'd have to put back together piece by piece. A hole so big that when you breathe in, it burns and makes you ache all over. One that makes you beg for someone to show you mercy, even if no one will because they all feel the same way as you. And was I ever really healed, or did I wake-up one morning and decide that I needed to move on?"

"It does take time to heal, Ryley, and everyone has to do it at their own pace."

I laugh out loud and adjust the way I'm sitting. I wish I hadn't worn a dress today, but Lois insisted, and I'm at a point in my life where I just do as she says, so I put on a yellow sundress and pulled my hair into a blue ribbon. That's as good as it gets for me right now. But sitting here, I want to be in sweats. I want my white socks covering my bare toes, and I want to be buried under an oversized sweatshirt. I want to hide.

"Time is my enemy. Time is the one thing I don't have and can't afford to lose. Time…" I shake my head and look toward the window. I bite my lip and close my eyes. My mind is blank. I refuse to see their images. I don't want to look, or remember. "I need to find a way to stop time or reverse it." I nod. "Reversing time would be ideal. If I could do that, I wouldn't be sitting here right now. My life… it'd be on the path that I created, that I worked hard for, but it's not. I'm standing in the center of the Interstate with traffic coming at me from both directions waiting… desperately waiting for someone or something to change everything that has happened in the last six years. So no, time doesn't heal anything. It just prolongs the hurt and pain.

"It sounds like you've had a lot to deal with, maybe more than others. Do you find solace in your friends?"

I shake my head. "I have two very close friends. One is from high school, she and her husband moved down here once the twins where stationed here. The other is a military wife. Any other friends I had bailed. I'm sure they didn't bail because of me, but because of the military. You move on, ya know? They don't want to associate…" I stop and think about that word. "Associate isn't the correct word; it's fear. They see what I went through and fear rips through their bodies, and they do what their bodies tell them: fight or flight. They all chose flight because they're all afraid they'll go through the same thing one day."

"What else do you experience from your friends and family?"

Easy question. "Pity. I got so sick and tired of the hugs and the pats on the shoulder. The looks—those were never-ending. I didn't need to see the pity in their eyes as they went from looking at me to looking at my belly. Everyone is sorry, but what exactly are they sorry for? Are they sorry that they voted for the people who sent our military to war? Are they sorry that their children aren't out defending our country? What are they sorry for?" My voice rises with my last question. I want to know. What goes through someone's mind when they tell you they're sorry that your loved one has died?

"I always want to ask why. Why are you sorry? Did you do something that I'm not aware of? Did you pull the trigger or supply the enemy with equipment to do harm? No, I didn't think so. Thing is, all the pity looks are back and each one brings me to my knees because guess what? They're all sorry again, and this time it's not going to matter what decision I make. Someone will be hurt. For that, they can be sorry."

"Ryley, I'm going to ask you again why are you here today?"

For the first time since I walked in the door, I look at the therapist. Her hair is cut short, framing her face. It's brown, but muted. There's no vibrancy to her color. It's dull and outdated, much like her couch. Her white, long-sleeved shirt is buttoned high, as if it wants to choke the life out of her. Her cat-like glasses perch on the edge of her nose, and she reclines in her chair with her pad of paper resting on her lap, her pen poised to write down my words at a moment's notice.

"I'm here because six years ago I lost the love of my life, but now he's back from the dead, and in a few weeks I'm set to marry my best friend. His brother."

Available Now

ACKNOWLEDGMENTS

This thank you goes out to every single one of my readers and future ones. Without you, writing couldn't be possible for me. Some people say that authors are their rockstars, but I think it is *you* who are the rockstars. Thank you for being awesome.

Also, I have to thank my husband for putting up with me. He has to deal with me when I get into my writing zone and I know that can't be easy.

And of course, I can't forget Kim Walker, the superpower PA. I swear she has the capability to do anything. I really do think she has powers. I would be lost without her.

Regina Wamba, is one amazing woman behind the camera. Thank you for making my photo shoot epic. You totally rocked the pictures and made an awesome cover out of them.

To my lovely editor, Victoria Schmitz, thank you for making my words shine. I don't know what I'd do without you.

To one of my favorite authors and friend, Heidi McLaughlin, thank you for always being there for me. I look forward to our future projects. Also, I owe you big time for lending me your lovely helpers: Kelli, Veronica,

Amy, Tammy, and Audrey. They have been such a huge help.

Lastly, I want to say thank you to the handsome model on the cover, Josh McCann. He did a great job being my Jason Avery.

Made in the USA
Charleston, SC
28 September 2016